Case of the Missing Marine

Corgi Case Files, Book 14

By

J.M. Poole

Sign up for Jeffrey's newsletter to get
all the latest corgi news—
AuthorJMPoole.com

CONTENTS

Mysteries by J.M. Poole

CORGI CASE FILES

CORGI CASE FILES

CASE OF THE

MISSING MARINE

BOOK 14

J.M. POOLE

Secret Staircase Books

Case of the Missing Marine
Published by Secret Staircase Books, an imprint of
Columbine Publishing Group, LLC
PO Box 416, Angel Fire, NM 87710

Book layout and design by Secret Staircase Books
Cover image © Felipe de Barros

First trade paperback edition: October, 2021
First e-book edition: October, 2021***
Publisher's Cataloging-in-Publication Data

Poole, J.M.
Case of the Missing Marine / by J.M. Poole.
p. cm.
ISBN 978-1649140623 (paperback)
ISBN 978-1649140630 (e-book)

1. Zachary Anderson (Fictitious character)--Fiction. 2. London, England
—Fiction. 3. Amateur sleuth—Fiction. 4. Pet detectives—Fiction. I. Title

Corgi Case Files Mystery Series : Book 14.
Poole, J.M., Corgi Case Files mysteries.

BISAC : FICTION / Mystery & Detective.

813/.54

ACKNOWLEDGMENTS

Beta readers, family members, and friends … there are always people to thank when writing a book. In this case, I'd like to thank my Posse members who helped read for me: Jason, Carol M, Michelle, Diane, Caryl, and Louise! Then, on the Secret Staircase Books' side of things, there is another set of readers: Marcia, Sandra, Susan, Paula, and Isobel!

A quick word about the Tower of London. Yes, this is the home of the Crown Jewels, and if you're ever in the area, they are worth checking out. However, don't use this book as a street guide. Yes, I've been to see the jewels, but no, the order in which they are displayed are not the same as in the book. Sorry 'bout that. No hate mail, please!

Also, as long as we're talking about London, you'll more than likely notice I used real street names and places. The walk from Buckingham Palace back to the hotel? That's the same route my wife and I walked. But, not all locations are real, and I took a few liberties.

And finally, I'd like to thank you, the reader. With your support, the adventures of our fun-loving trio will not be stopping anytime soon! Happy reading!

J.

For Giliane —

At long last, we're getting out of the hot country and headed north! The Pacific NW is calling our name!

ONE

Did you have any idea book signings could be so exciting? The last few days happened so fast that they were practically a blur. Didn't you think so, Zachary?"

"You have no idea. I've only done one other book signing, and I'll tell you what, it had *nothing* on this last one. Crowds of people, poisonings, elements of voodoo, and some really good food. You know what? I can't complain."

"Would you do another?" my fiancée asked.

"What, another signing? Wow, that's a good question. I'm still not fond of them, but to be honest, I had no idea how many fans I had out there. Plus, with *Heart of Éire*, I've seen a serious uptick in sales from my other titles, so I guess yeah, if MCU wanted me to do another signing, I'd do it."

"But … under your terms, right?" Jillian asked.

I nodded. "Of course. It definitely helps to have a group of friends with me to help spend the time. I don't like the idea of sitting by myself behind a table."

"There were thousands of people there," Jillian recalled. "They all wanted to meet you. And don't forget the podcast! The girl who hosted it said the number of her fans nearly tripled overnight, thanks to you being on her show."

Before I get ahead of myself, I suppose a little context would be in order. My name is Zachary Anderson, but everyone calls me Zack. I live in southwestern Oregon, in a little town called Pomme Valley, or PV for short. It's a town of less than five thousand people, but thankfully, we have every amenity we could need right next door, in Medford: exceptional restaurants, a small airport which several big-name airlines use, and just about every store one would need. Add in the fact that it was less than ten minutes away, and you've got yourself an ideal location to settle down. Oh, I should also mention that this area is known for its wineries, seeing how the small town of PV has over twenty, and that includes mine. Lentari Cellars is the local favorite, and I can proudly state that a simple bottle of Syrah from my winery can easily fetch over a hundred dollars a bottle.

But wait, there's more!

I'm also a writer. My genre of choice? Romance. Scoff if you will, but I can tell you that romance books are popular right now, and will continue for quite some time. As such, it's the perfect genre to develop a strong fan base. Romance readers are voracious. They will easily purchase any book with your name on it, and will pre-order any titles that you might have available, no questions asked. But, I will also state, for the record, that you won't find my name on any books I have published. I prefer to use a nom de plume, and in this case, it's Chastity Wadsworth.

Let the teasing begin.

Yes, I know it's a female name, and yes, I encourage people to think I'm a woman behind the keyboard. However, more and more people are learning that there's a man behind that name, and do you know what? It hasn't negatively affected my sales. In fact, because of recent events, and the simple fact my name keeps popping up all over the Internet, my sales have never been stronger.

Now that we're caught up, I can ... no, wait. I forgot a profession. That's the problem with wearing too many hats. I'm bound to forget one.

I'm also a police consultant. I help out the local police department whenever something happens that they can't explain. Well, specifically, they ask for my dogs' help. I know that sounds unorthodox, but let me assure you, Sherlock and Watson have solved a variety of cases for the PVPD. What kinds? Well, everything from murder, to locating missing persons, to recovering stolen merchandise. Those two little corgis are PVPD's secret weapon.

Now, back to the present.

Walking in with me, to my house on my vineyard, is my lovely fiancée, Jillian Cooper. As was mentioned earlier, we were just returning home from a book signing in New Orleans for my most recent release which, oddly enough, wasn't a romance. Instead, it was a period piece set in 19th century Ireland. This particular book was inspired by my good friend Vance Samuelson, and his wife Tori. Vance had asked me to write his wife into one of my books, essentially naming a character after her, but I did him one better: a brand new story set in Tori's favorite country. When *Heart of Éire* was published, I will admit to being curious how it would sell, seeing how it was a stand-alone title, and in a genre I have never touched before. Yet, much to my amazement, the book was burning up the charts, and even hitting the ever elusive *New York Times* best seller list. It was my first time ever, and I couldn't be prouder. That was the book I promoted when we went to New Orleans. And *that* was what we were just returning home from. I should say we were tired, spent, and just wanted to crash, but thanks to a last-minute text Jillian had received while we were in New Orleans, we were far from exhausted. We had both chatted non-stop the entire trip home.

"I just want to know how he got his hands on it in the first place," I wondered again, as I wheeled both of our suitcases inside the door and left them propped up against the wall. "If he's the one who sent it to me, that means Joshua was in Wales. What in the world was he doing there? And, more importantly, how did he get his hands on that silver chest? Hey, Sherlock? Watson? Are you two hungry? Here, let me get you guys some kibble."

"I'll get them a fresh bowl of water," Jillian added.

While the dogs munched away on their dinner, Jillian sank down on a seat at the kitchen table while I procured a couple of bottles of water for ourselves.

"Are you certain that *heading under* is code for *I'm in trouble*?"

Jillian pulled out her cell phone and, probably for the tenth time since she received it, showed me the message on the display:

OUT OF TIME. HEADNG UNDER. REMBR CHST.

I tapped the screen. "See? Chest, I get. He's reminding us about the silver chest from Ireland. He … no?"

Jillian was shaking her head. "Yes, I can see how you would say that, and CHST does look like it's short for *chest*."

"What else could it mean?" I asked.

"When we were little," Jillian began, as a wistful look appeared on her face, "the two of us would play these games where we'd always ask each other *what if*. What if he was an astronaut and I was a scientist? Or, what if we were both race car drivers, competing against each other? We'd invent daring scenarios just to see how the other would react to it."

I shrugged. "Most kids did stuff like that when they were little. Myself included. It's just using your imagination."

Jillian nodded. "That's true. However, one of Joshua's favorite imaginary professions was being a super-spy, like James Bond."

I raised a hand. "Same, here. What boy hasn't dreamed of taking on the bad guys, getting the girl, and saving the world?"

"Well, yes, his text message could be reminding us about the silver chest from Ireland. In fact, I think he deliberately worded it like that in case his message was intercepted by ... well, let's call them *unfriendly* eyes."

"But you think it means something else?" I guessed.

Jillian nodded. "I do. At least, I think I do. I don't know, Zachary. Do you think I'm reading too much into it?"

"Well, what do you think it means?" I gently asked.

Jillian tapped her phone and looked at the message that was still displayed. "Remember chest. Or, more specifically, *CHST*. C — H — S — T. The only reason I'm thinking of this is because the one thing Joshua had a habit of saying, in case things were not going the way he had planned, was *chips have started tumbling*."

"Chips have started tumbling," I repeated, thinking. "As in, things are starting to happen which won't be good?"

"That's what I've always believed. Joshua has used that saying so many times that I'm just sure it was meant for me, letting me know whatever he's doing, things aren't going as planned."

I nodded. "All right, I can buy that. So, what do you think? Do we need to check up on him? You said he's in the Marines?"

"That's right."

"Then, our next step should be easy. I say we call up his commander and make sure everything is all right. Hopefully, this will be just one huge misunderstanding. You said he's currently working with MI6? That means he's over in England. Wales is part of the UK, so I think it's not too far off the ... are we expecting anyone?"

Surprised, Jillian leaned forward to rest her hands on the kitchen table. From there, we could both look out the breakfast nook windows and get a great view of the driveway. In this manner, we watched a sleek-looking black sedan, with heavily tinted windows, pull into our driveway and coast to a stop. Curious as to the make of the car, I stared at the logo, but couldn't place it. Wings? What car manufacturer used wings for their logo?

That's when I noticed the complete absence of noise. Startled, I looked over at Sherlock and Watson, who were sitting in the doorway leading from the kitchen to the living room. Both had their tongues out, and neither looked concerned in the slightest. Why weren't they losing their minds? Most dog owners will back me up when I say that, whenever a stranger pulls up to your house, your dogs will typically go bonkers. My two corgis will usually raise their hackles and turn into demon dogs if you come up to this house unannounced. But, this time? Not a peep.

"I wonder why they aren't barking," Jillian murmured, noticing the same thing I had. "We're so isolated out here, they can usually hear someone coming from several miles away. Look, did you see that? Sherlock just looked at the door. He knows someone is out there, yet he's not barking. Is he okay?"

I squatted next to the dogs and draped an arm around the two of them. "Guys? Is everything okay? You do know that a strange car just pulled into the drive, don't you? Why aren't you barking your fool heads off?"

The doorbell chimed loudly, causing both me and Jillian to jump. Much to my amazement, neither dog barked a single warning. There were no woofs, or howls, or whining. What did their Royal Canineships do? Rise to their feet, give themselves a good stretch and a shake, and slowly make their way to the door.

"I feel like I should be humming the *Twilight Zone* theme right about now," I joked, as I started for the door. Looking back at Jillian, I inclined my head at her phone. "Are you going to try and reach Joshua's commander?"

Jillian nodded. "I'm not exactly certain who I can call, but I do have a few friends in the military. I'll start with them."

"You do that. I'll ..." The doorbell rang again.

By this time, the dogs were sitting complacently in the foyer as they waited for me to arrive. Dogs. I'll never figure them out. "I'll take care of this. I shouldn't be long."

I pushed by the dogs, who were still on their best behavior, and opened the door. A tall, impeccably dressed older man was standing before me. He was wearing a tailored black suit, tapered at the waist. The jacket, I couldn't help but notice, was close-fitting, had flapped pockets with an additional ticket pocket, and had high arm holes. What did all of that mean?

The suit was British. I know, 'cause Jillian told me later, after I described it for her.

"Are you Mr. Zachary Anderson?" the man in black politely asked. He had an accent. British, I believe.

I nodded. "I am. And you are?"

"Here to personally deliver this to you. Good day to you, sir. Ah, such cute dogs. I've always been fond of Her Majesty the Queen's favorites."

With that, the stranger handed me a thick envelope, bowed once, and turned on his heel. Within moments, the large black sedan roared back to life and disappeared down my driveway, but not before I finally noticed the make of the car. It was an Aston Martin. I later learned it was one of the premier luxury cars manufactured in Britain. That should have been my first tip-off, but if you're familiar with my history, you'll know I'm not always the sharpest tool in the shed.

Still holding the envelope in my hand, I turned to Jillian and gave her a questioning stare, but she was facing the opposite direction and talking to someone using an urgent tone. Deciding to let her be for the time being, I headed back to the kitchen table and inspected the envelope I had been given.

Sliding my finger along the seam like I've done to countless other envelopes almost had me snapping my finger completely off at the knuckle. The paper that was used for this particular envelope had to be eighty-pound cardstock. Additionally, there was tape, not adhesive, sealing the envelope, and it refused to break. I was going to have to cut this one open.

Turning back to Jillian, I could tell she wasn't close to finishing this particular call, and since this envelope was addressed to me, and I was determined to shield Jillian from any potential bad news, the envelope was opened.

Inside was a thick, pale piece of parchment that had a red castle imprinted and centered on the top with a caption of Windsor Castle directly below. Skimming through the letter, I felt the blood drain from my face as I realized who had sent it, and why. Turning to see Jillian just finishing up her call, I noticed her face was the same color as mine.

That couldn't be good.

"Zachary?" Jillian began, as she hurried over to me. "You're not going to believe this. Joshua ... wait, are you all right? You look as pale as I feel. What did that man want?"

I shook my head. "Nuh-uh. You first, then I'll tell you about mine. Joshua? Is he okay?"

Jillian shook her head. "He's currently missing. Oh, what do you think has happened to him, Zachary? Do you think he's in some kind of trouble?"

"Do we know what he was doing over there?" I asked, completely forgetting about the letter I was holding.

"I was finally able to reach someone who identified himself as a Sergeant Major. The only thing he could tell me was Joshua had been collaborating with MI6, and if I had any further questions, then I should contact them. I don't like this one bit."

"Are you going to try and reach someone from MI6?" I asked. "I mean, is that even possible?"

Jillian shrugged. "We're about to find out. What about you? What are you holding?"

I held up the paper and tapped the red logo at the top. "Oh, nothing really, but a personal invitation for an audience with Her Majesty, the Queen of England."

Jillian's mouth fell open. "Wh-what?"

I passed the paper over. "It would seem Queen Elizabeth II would like to meet Sherlock and Watson and personally thank them for helping solve one of their oldest cold cases."

"That's so amazing! Does she indicate when this should happen?"

I took the paper back and skimmed through it. "Well, I don't see anything about it. Perhaps we should …?"

Jillian's cell started to ring, which was why I had trailed off. Snatching up her phone, Jillian eagerly took the call.

"Hello? Yes, this is Jillian Cooper. Who is this? Oh. Umm, I'm pleased to meet you, Staff Sergeant." She muted the call. "Zachary! It's someone from MI6! Wow, how did they know I was looking for answers?"

"You called the Marines first, didn't you?" I whispered, forgetting no one on the phone could hear me. "They must have let MI6 know you called."

"That was less than five minutes ago! How could they …? I … I'm sorry? No, I'm here. I'm on my cell, so I apologize if the connection isn't the greatest. Joshua? He's my brother. I'm just trying to … no, there's no family emergency. Why am I calling? Well …"

"Tell him you were expecting a phone call, and it never happened," I whispered.

"… it's just that … what was that? Oh. I'm so sorry. That was Zachary, my fiancé. Listen, I, er, it's just that …"

I watched Jillian's eyes fill and I knew she wouldn't be able to finish the call. Before she completely broke down in sobs, I reached out and gently took the phone from her.

"Hello, there. I'm sorry about that. This is Zachary Anderson, stepping in for Jillian."

"What happened to Ms. Cooper?" a patient, but firm, voice asked.

"She's very close to her brother," I explained. "She's worried about him. We get the impression something might've happened to him, and we were just looking for verification that he's okay. Umm, he is, isn't he?"

"The only thing I'm allowed to say, Mr. Anderson," the voice politely informed me, "is that First Sergeant Joshua Cooper didn't report in when he was supposed to."

"When was that?" I wanted to know.

"Last night. I have to ask how you knew to ask about First Sergeant Cooper? Have you been in contact with him?"

"I have not, no," I answered. "Can you tell me this? Was he stationed in the UK?"

"He was stationed in London," the voice confirmed. "He's had frequent collaborations with various intelligence groups."

"Would one of those be MI6?" I asked.

"That information is classified."

"Are your people looking for him?"

"As much as we're able to, yes."

I looked over at Jillian. "Is there anything else you want me to ask him?"

"Just tell him to please find my brother. I'm really starting to worry about him."

"She says ..."

"I heard her," the voice said. "We're doing our best. Good day to you, sir."

The line went dead.

"Did they say anything else?" Jillian asked,

hopeful.

"No, I'm sorry. Whoever I was talking to confirmed his people were looking for him, but he wouldn't give me any other details than that."

"Was he able to confirm that Joshua was working with MI6?"

"Not really," I said, shaking my head. "Then again, he didn't deny it, either."

"Did he say *what* he was working on?"

"Classified," I said, shaking my head.

My fiancée let out a heavy sigh. "I have a bad feeling about this."

I held up the paper. "Look, we've been invited to Buckingham Palace. That's in England. Correct me if I'm wrong, but isn't the headquarters for MI6 also in England? More specifically, London?"

Jillian's eyes widened. "It is."

"I say we kill two birds with one stone."

"What about the dogs?" Jillian wanted to know.

"They're coming with us," I stated. "The Queen specifically stated she wanted to meet the two of them, remember? That means they get to go along."

"Aren't there strict regulations in place for animals entering a foreign country?" Jillian asked, frowning. "Let me see. I … yes, here it is. Okay, this is good. It says here that the dogs don't have to go through quarantine."

"That's good," I decided.

"But, they need to be microchipped …"

"Which they are," I said.

"… and be vaccinated against Rabies …"

"Which they are," I repeated.

"… and have all their vaccination records …"

"Which we do. Somewhere in here. Look at the time. There's no way Harry's clinic is still open at this time. I can probably have him fax the records to wherever they need to go."

"… and finally, they need to have been treated for tapeworm."

"What? Ew. We don't have time for that!"

"It says the dogs are supposed to have this test done no earlier than five days before entering the UK."

"Hmm, that's going to be a problem. I'm going to have to ask Harry about that."

Harrison Watt was one of my closest friends, and he just also happened to be Pomme Valley's town veterinarian.

"Do you have any idea how long a flight it is to London?" Jillian asked.

"Five or six hours?" I guessed, hopeful I had rounded up and not down.

"I'm pretty sure the closest direct, non-stop flight to London is from Seattle. Let me check." Jillian quickly pulled her phone out and started tapping in instructions. "It's a long flight. Nine and a half hours, and yes, it's from Seattle. If we leave from here, heading east, then we're looking at a minimum of fourteen hours of travel time, seeing how we'll have a layover *somewhere*."

"Tickets aren't gonna come cheap," I groaned.

"Fine. Let's see what we can get to … what is it?"

Jillian pointed at the envelope. "Why does it look like there's something else in there?"

I shook my head. "It's heavy paper. It just looks like there is…"

Jillian took the envelope, hefted it in her hand, then checked inside. Much to my surprise, she pulled out what looked like a skinny checkbook, but turned out to be a number of what looked like four inch by eight inch papers stapled together. You have probably already figured out what they were, but for me, I was a little slow on the uptake.

"Are those …?"

Jillian nodded. "They're tickets. It looks like Her Majesty has invited us over on her dime. Or pence, I guess."

"Why are there so many?" I wanted to know.

Jillian counted the slips. "There are eight. Let's see. Two for you and two for me."

"That's only four," I pointed out.

She then held up two sets of two slips each. "Mm-hmm, and this is for Sherlock, and this one is Watson's. Look! It would seem Her Majesty the Queen has some pull with the travel regulations. It says on their tickets *Records Exempt*. Does that mean we don't have to worry about that tapeworm test?"

"I sure hope so," I murmured. "Wow. She bought the dogs tickets. That was incredibly nice of her."

"Well, to be fair, she *does* want to meet them,"

Jillian pointed out. "And I'd also like to mention that nowhere on this sheet of paper does it say she'd like to meet us, too."

I shrugged. "Get used to it. I did. They'll always be more popular than us."

"We need to pack!"

I pointed at our two suitcases, which were waiting just inside the door. "We already are."

"You know what I mean. We need clean clothes. Hurry, Zachary. Grab some clean things and then we'll run by my place so I can do the same."

I know by now you are probably thinking that Jillian and I are living together. Granted, the two of us spent so much time in each other's company that we practically did, only we still had separate houses. I haven't quite figured out what to do about that yet. Jillian lives in one of PV's historic houses, Carnation Cottage. Her house is gorgeous, spacious, and I wish I could simply pick the thing up and move it here. After all, my house is on my winery, and it's sitting on more than fifty acres of land. That, in itself, is incredibly appealing, since that meant our nearest neighbor couldn't possibly be able to look through their windows into one of ours.

As for what to do about the houses, that would have to wait until after the wedding. Then again, we have each been delaying the ceremony for long enough, citing various reasons. The most common seems to be finding the right time, as well as the right venue, since we have a lot of people to invite. Not for the first time have I considered having just a simple, private ceremony with close friends, then inviting the whole town for the reception. The problem with that has not changed: where to hold it. Jillian knows *everybody* in town, and because of that, there are only so many places we could choose from.

However, that wasn't what was holding us back from picking a date. You see, we've been waiting to hear from Jillian's brother. My fiancée isn't about to get married without her only brother in attendance. Joshua had a busy schedule and everyone knew it. Therefore, people knew we were waiting for the right moment. After all, Jillian and I have been together for a while now, and yet, he's the only person in her family I haven't met. Our schedules just haven't allowed for it yet.

For now, it'll have to wait yet again. This time, we have legitimate reasons, namely, we have to rush to the United Kingdom and see if we can figure out what has happened to Joshua. And, at the same time, we'll have to make some time for the Queen, seeing how she's the one making this particular trip possible.

Hmm, maybe we can use our new-found fame with the Queen to our advantage? After all, Josh was working with MI6 when he disappeared. Perhaps we could get some royal assistance? It was definitely worth a try.

Throwing my dirty clothes into the clothes hamper and hastily selecting a clean batch from dresser and closet, I turned to Jillian, who was sitting quietly on the bed.

"Penny for your thoughts?"

Jillian looked up. "I was just thinking."

"About your brother?"

"Yes. It feels like in the last five years, I've barely seen him."

"And I was just thinking that, of all the time I've lived here, and since you and I have been together, I have yet to meet him. He always seems to be busy, or else his leave is revoked and he ends up canceling on us. The two of you were … er, *are* close, aren't you?"

"Yes. We share many similarities. We both love sci-fi stories. We both love puzzles. We both love the same type of movies."

"How many years older is he?"

"Four. He's always been there for me. I guess that's why I feel I need to be there for him."

"Because of this one text," I said.

"Yes. I know it's silly, Zachary. England is a long way away. You don't need to go. I can do this by myself."

"What self-respecting guy is going to allow that?" I demanded, as I continued to throw various things into my suitcase. "Absolutely not. He's your family, which makes him part of my family. Where you go, I go, too."

"Thank you."

"So, tell me about Josh," I said. "What does he like to do? Do you know what he was doing for the military?"

Jillian shrugged. "What I can tell you is that he's incredibly gifted at breaking codes. Perhaps that had something to do with it?"

"Cryptography?" I guessed.

"Yes."

"That shouldn't surprise me," I chuckled.

"Why do you say that?" Jillian asked.

"Well, think about it. He sent me the silver box. And as you are well aware, it turned out to be anything *but* just a box. I don't know how he got his hands on it, but clearly something about it caught his fancy. Maybe he knew what was inside?"

"He probably had his suspicions," Jillian conceded.

I shrugged. "Either way you look at it, whatever he was doing, he stumbled across the chest and knew he had to get rid of it. Makes you wonder, doesn't it?"

Jillian's soft brown eyes met my own. "What? What does it make you wonder?"

"What *else* he might know about."

That one statement brought Jillian up short.

"Are you suggesting Joshua was involved in some illegal scheme?"

I threw up my hands in surrender. "Absolutely not. That's not what I'm saying at all. What I meant was, what if the military has him working on some secret, undercover mission? Perhaps he came into possession of the silver chest while working one of these cases?"

Jillian finally nodded. "I guess it's possible. We won't really know unless one of his superiors confirms it ..."

"... which sounds like they won't," I interjected.

"... or else we hear it from his own mouth."

Having finished throwing a selection of clean clothes into my suitcase, I moved on to the dogs. If they were going to accompany us on a long flight like that, in the cabin with us, then we needed to be prepared. Hurrying over to the storage closet located near my kitchen and dedicated to the dogs, I hastily assembled the necessary items: toys, chewies, treats, disposable bags, pre-moistened paper towels. Their kibble was dumped into a resealable plastic bag, and several bottles of water were slid into the pockets on either side of the bag.

"Nuh-uh," Jillian said, shaking her head. "Those water bottles won't make it on the plane. They'll never make it through security."

"I can't bring water for them?" I asked, bewildered.

"You can, but you have to buy it from the stores on the other side of the security checkpoint."

"Which means I'll have to pay exorbitant prices, won't I?"

Jillian held up her hands in a helpless manner. "I don't make the rules. They do."

"What a racket," I grumbled. "What do they think I'm gonna do with it? Throw water at the flight attendants?"

"We'll buy more when we're through," Jillian

promised. "That reminds me. What about Sherlock and Watson?"

"What about them?" I wanted to know, as I zipped the stuffed-to-the-gills-doggie-backpack up.

"What if they have to go to the bathroom?"

"I think they have places for the pets to go inside the airport."

"No, on the plane."

"You think the dogs are going to go potty on board?"

"Zachary, it's over nine hours. Do you think you can hold it for that long?"

"I sure as heck plan on trying," I vowed. "Those airplane lavatories are disgusting."

"Think about them. You don't want them to have an accident, do you?"

"True. You make a fine point. Hey, here's what we'll do."

I returned to the dogs' closet and started fumbling through the things on the top shelf.

"What are you looking for?"

I held up a stack of what looked like white padded envelopes.

"These. These will be perfect. Thank you. That would have been awkward."

"Puppy pads!" Jillian exclaimed. "Brilliant! Do you think they'll use them?"

I looked down at my two corgis. Both were looking at the pads in my hand and together, as one, they turned to look at me as if I had just suggested

I should put diapers on them.

"Oh, knock it off, you two," I scolded. "Jillian is right. You're going to be happy I have these, mark my words."

In less than twenty-four hours, I was proven right. Not only did the dogs end up using them, but each of the dogs made me take them to the tiny bathroom on the plane—twice—during our flight. Thankfully, our tickets were for first class, so each of us sat next to a dog and watched as the flight crew made cooing noises at them every time they passed.

But, what was most remarkable was that, for once, I was right. I had correctly guessed Joshua's mission, only it really wasn't cause for celebration. If I was right, it meant every intelligence agency on the planet would love to get their hands on him.

TWO

A ll I can say is it's a good thing I'm not claustrophobic. That's way too long to be cooped up in an airplane."

"Can you imagine what it would've been like in coach?" Jillian asked, as we shuffled along in the long line of people waiting to go through customs. "We seriously need to thank the Queen when we see her. I don't usually fly first class, seeing how it's so much more expensive, but now? I think I'm hooked. What about you, Zachary?"

I shrugged. "For long flights? I can get on board, pardon the pun. Those price tags, though, are something else. The Queen had to have dropped a lot of money on those tickets."

We looked down at the dogs. Surprisingly, both of the corgis had been on their best behavior for the flight. Sherlock exhibited some signs of discomfort as we began our descent, but a good ear rub solved that problem. As for potty breaks, those puppy pads worked like a charm! I've never trained either of the dogs on how to use them, and I wasn't too sure they wouldn't turn their noses up. However, walking them down the aisle, on our way to the lavatory, I could only pray that I wouldn't be asking the flight attendants for a bottle of cleaner. In this case, as soon as the pad was spread out on the floor, both dogs did their business.

We ended up repeating that particular potty procedure twice.

"You owe them some treats," Jillian reminded me, as we headed out after being cleared through customs. "And, I can't tell you how much I appreciated those two little words on the dogs' tickets. *Records Exempt.* You'd think it said the dogs were to be treated like royalty. How are you feeling, Zachary?"

"Are you asking if I'm jet-lagged? A little. However, this is England and I love traveling. Plus, it's overcast and looks like it could drizzle at any moment. Yep, look at that. Everyone is driving on the wrong side of the road. It doesn't get any better than this!"

It *could* have been better. The airlines, in their supreme brilliance, lost my garment bag. Oh, I have plenty of clothes in my regular suitcase, but the garment bag? It had the best suit I owned in it. After all, we were due to meet Her Majesty, so it was only proper to dress appropriately. Thankfully, most airlines manage to not only find lost luggage at an incredible pace, but deliver said luggage to wherever the owner happened to be staying. So, I wasn't worried. Yet.

Jillian pointed east. "We need to head that way. I see people getting in and out of those black cabs over there."

"Roger that. Sherlock? Watson? Come on, guys."

Once we were tucked away inside a cab and were headed out into the city, I gave Jillian a nudge.

"What's the name of our hotel?"

"I sent you pictures of all our reservations," Jillian teased. "We're going to have to do something about that memory of yours. Let me see your phone. See? Here it is: Conrad London St. James."

"Have you been to London before?" I asked, as I sat back in my seat.

Sherlock jumped on my lap and promptly settled down. Watson appeared next and wedged herself in between me and Jillian. Dogs.

"Twice before," Jillian admitted. "Michael and I came here once, so we could visit Stonehenge."

"And the second?" I prompted.

"It was not long after Michael's death. I was feeling low, and some friends suggested that I pack an overnight bag and do something I typically wouldn't."

"Meaning, take a trip to another continent, huh?"

My fiancée nodded. "It was the last thing I wanted to do, but I could also see that I was slipping into a dark place. So, I grabbed a few friends and we all flew out here for the weekend. Considering the travel time, it was a very short trip, but I will also say it was incredibly therapeutic. What about you?"

"I've been here just one other time. Samantha and I stopped here on our way to our first cruise."

"Where did you go?" Jillian asked, as her body leaned into mine when the cabbie took a roundabout at what felt like a hundred miles an hour.

"It was a cruise along the Adriatic," I recalled. "If memory serves, we departed from Greece and finished in Barcelona. There were stops in Italy and Montenegro. It was my one and only cruise with Samantha."

"Is that why you shied away from taking another cruise?" Jillian asked, as she took my hand in hers. "Painful memories?"

I sighed and gave her hand a squeeze. "Yeah, I suppose it is. I didn't want to start thinking about Sam if I was going on a cruise with you."

"We had a great time in Alaska," Jillian reminded me. "I don't think you need to worry about that anymore."

I put my arm around her and pulled her close. "True story."

Thirty minutes later, we pulled up to our hotel, only to my eyes, the Conrad London St. James looked more like a series of row houses, set in alternating colors. The hotel's front entrance sat under an overhang, and once an attendant saw the four of us exiting our cab, he hurried out to take our bags.

"Welcome to the Conrad London!" a young man of thirty exclaimed. "We're so glad to welcome you to our ... oh! Corgis! How adorable!"

Sherlock and Watson looked up at the friendly bellhop and waggled their stumpy tails. Reaching into my doggie backpack, I retrieved two treats and handed them to the young kid.

"Here. This is for them. Give them these and they'll be your friends for life."

The treats were tentatively held out to the dogs, who immediately sat. Sherlock even lifted a paw, as if he expected a paw-shake was necessary to secure his goodie. But, before either of the dogs took their treats, their noses lifted and I was certain they were moments away from letting out a few warning woofs. That's when I noticed both Sherlock and Watson were staring at the bellhop's outstretched hand, as though they suddenly thought they were being given broccoli. I say that word because, last week, Jillian had dropped a floret on the floor and, when neither of us warned them they couldn't have it, the two corgis raced each other to see who could eat the offending item first. From the look Sherlock gave me, since he was the winner and had immediately scooped up the broccoli into his mouth, he must've thought I was the devil incarnate for offering such a morsel. It was promptly spit out and even Watson, who sniffed a few times at the item, wouldn't touch it.

I only wish I had been recording it.

After a few moments, both dogs lost interest

in whatever had caught their attention and took their treats. At the same time, I surreptitiously snapped a photo on my phone. If you're wondering why, well, I've long since learned to pay attention to whatever catches these two's attention. Since we were here to (mainly) figure out what happened to Jillian's brother, I decided we were working a case, and therefore, taking pictures of the corgi clues, as I call them. Inevitably, when we review the pictures at a future date, they will make sense in some fashion. For now, the only thing I accomplished was looking creepy, which Jillian thought was incredibly funny.

When both dogs had finished their treats, the kid looked up at me.

"I've always loved corgis. I think these are the first two I've ever met up close. What are their names?"

"That one is Sherlock and the other is Watson."

"Oh? How clever! Will you be staying with us long?"

I turned to Jillian, who shrugged. "We're here at least three days."

"You might be with us longer?" the uniformed staff member anxiously asked.

"Anything's possible," I returned. "In this case, I strongly doubt it."

Days from now, when I looked back at this moment, I realized that *this* was when I jinxed myself. I'm sure of it. When was I going to learn to keep my big trap shut? Not only was I wrong, I was *really* wrong. More on that later.

Properly checked in, and with both dogs stretched out on the bed, as though they were the ones who'd signed for the room, we unpacked our luggage. The room certainly wasn't the largest we've ever been in, and it was far from the tiniest, but considering how we booked it at the last minute, it would do. The king bed was on the left wall, and there was a small desk facing the perimeter wall, beneath the window. Jillian pulled out the desk's chair and sank down on it.

"I'm ashamed to say that I thought I'd handle the jet lag better."

"It's catching up to you, isn't it?" I guessed.

"It is. I …"

Jillian trailed off as there was a knock on the door. Alarmed, I looked over at the corgis, since the last thing I wanted was to have both of them barking their heads off. Yet again, though, the two of them seemingly ignored the intrusion and allowed us humans to deal with the problem. Promising myself I'd get them in to see Harry, my good friend who just so happens to be Pomme Valley's town veterinarian, I headed for the door.

Expecting to see a member of the hotel's staff, I was surprised to find a guy, younger than me, dressed in a long-sleeved blue business shirt and black slacks. He was also holding a leather satchel, straight out of the mystery shows Jillian and I like watching on television. Oh, to be thin and be able to pull off a look like that!

"Yes? Can I help you?"

"Are you Mr. Zachary Anderson? And you, miss? You are Miss Jillian Cooper?"

I shook the guy's outstretched hand. "I am, and she is. Who are you?"

"Oh, my apologies. Detective Sergeant Gary Lestrade, at your service. Yes, I know what you're thinking. It's not as if I don't hear it every day. At least, you will be, if you're familiar with Sir Arthur Conan Doyle."

Both Jillian and I had given a tiny, visible start when we recognized the name of the police inspector from the Sherlock Holmes stories. I turned to look at the dogs, who were still stretched out on the bed. Neither of them had so much as bared their teeth or let out even the softest of growls.

"You could say that. Back there? Those two are actually named Sherlock and Watson."

DS Lestrade didn't seem surprised by this bit of news. In fact, I got the impression that he already knew that. The young inspector nodded once and then faced me.

"My parents were huge fans of the stories, so naturally, I get to have a unique name. Sherlock and Watson. I love their names. If you don't mind my asking, what prompted you to name them after Britain's most famous fictional detectives?"

I ruffled Sherlock's fur. "Well, he was already named when I got him. As for Watson, well, I know it's not really a name for a girl, but it went with Sherlock, so there you have it."

"Watson is a *she*? You're right. It's not really a girl's name, is it?"

Jillian gave a slight cough. When DS Lestrade was looking her way, she gave the friendly policeman a smile.

"You said that you were informed our dogs were named Sherlock and Watson? Can I ask, by whom?"

"This information comes from the chief inspector," Lestrade explained. "He never disclosed where he got it."

"You're from Scotland Yard, aren't you?" I asked.

"Technically, I'm from the Metropolitan Police, but it's often been referred to as Scotland Yard. Well, this would be the *New* Scotland Yard. I've been assigned as your liaison."

"You're *what*?" I asked, as I sat down on the bed next to my fiancée. "Why would New Scotland Yard assign someone to us? You said you're a detective sergeant? I can't imagine why they'd choose you to tag along with us."

"For the record, Mr. Anderson," Lestrade said, with a sheepish grin, "I've only recently earned my sergeant's stripes, which was last month, and I passed my detective exams on Monday."

"Well, congrats, pal," I told our new friend. "I don't know if it's a blessing or a curse, being saddled with us."

Lestrade laughed and held out a hand, toward the bed. "Would you mind? I'd like to meet your dogs, if that's all right. I feel like they should be included with all introductions. It's just a little quirk of mine."

Holy crap on a cracker! How could I have forgotten to introduce the dogs? Then again, why wasn't Sherlock voicing his displeasure at being ignored? Usually, the squat little fellow would let out a bark loud enough to pierce eardrums.

"I'm rather shocked he hasn't barked," Jillian said.

"You and me both. No barking for the doorbell, they were quiet when DS Lestrade knocked on the door, and now? I forget to introduce them and they don't make a peep."

"Is that a problem?" Lestrade wanted to know.

I hooked a thumb at the dogs. "You don't know these two. They are very *specific* about doing things just so, and if either of them deviate, then I usually book 'em a visit with my friend, the town veterinarian."

Jillian, still sitting beside me on the bed, leaned forward. "Wait a moment. If you're here, and you're here under orders, then that means someone knows why we're here, isn't that right?"

Lestrade shrugged. "Perhaps."

"Let's just drop the pretenses and move this right along," I decided. Leveling a look at our new friend, I lowered my voice, as if I thought the room was bugged. Then again, since we never told them we were planning on visiting Europe, it very well could be the case. "We're here to find out what happened to her brother, First Sergeant Joshua Cooper. By any chance, do you have any information for us?"

DS Lestrade walked over to the desk, set his satchel on the surface, and unbuckled the clasp. Reaching inside, he retrieved a sheaf of papers, flipped through them to verify all were there, and then squared them up on the desk's surface. They were then presented to me.

"Here. I made copies of the files for you. Thought you might like to see them."

Interested, Jillian leaned over my shoulder to look at the pages. Since it was her brother, I automatically handed them to her. Sitting in silence, I watched as Jillian skimmed through the papers.

"It says here he's earned several commendations," Jillian began. "And, I can't help but notice how many reports are in here."

"Is that good or bad?" I asked.

"From what I see here, it's good. Apparently, New Scotland Yard thought highly of Joshua."

"He was a legend at cryptography," Lestrade finally said. "I only met him once. He was studying something called the Voynich manuscript."

Jillian nodded thoughtfully. "I've heard of it. It's a codex from the fifteenth century, and it uses an alphabet no one has been able to decipher. Wait, you're telling me Joshua was able to figure it out?"

Lestrade shrugged. "I don't know, I'm afraid."

"Oh, here it is," Jillian reported, as she flipped through a few more pages in the report. "No, it says he was working on it, but only in his free time."

"The dude works on uncrackable codes for fun," I muttered. "That's impressive."

"He spent a lot of time at the British Museum," Lestrade said. "Anyway, I can tell you your brother is an incredibly gifted cryptologist and researcher."

Jillian nodded. "I'm aware. There isn't anything Joshua couldn't do."

"May I have that back? Thank you. There, do you see this here? It says that your brother's work at breaking codes is what caught MI6's attention. They made an offer, he accepted, and the rest is, as they say, history."

I pointed at the report. "Could you please flip to the back and tell us what he was working on last?"

"If I did that, then I'd tell you what he was working on *first*."

"Their report must have it the other way around," Jillian explained. "Very well, what does it say on the top page? What was the most recent project he had been working on?"

Lestrade let the stack of papers flop back onto the pile. He studied the page for a few moments before shrugging. After a few moments, he handed the report back to Jillian.

"The report hasn't been filled out. The only thing on the page is a name of a storage facility. At least, I think that's what it is."

"A storage facility?" I asked. Just then, I noticed both dogs had perked up, showing the first signs of life since DS Lestrade had entered the room. Coincidence? "What's the name of it? What do we know about it?"

"Cryptex Solutions," Jillian said, as she read the name aloud.

Lestrade shrugged. "I personally haven't heard of it, but that's not saying much. I'm from Inverness, and only moved to London several months ago."

"Where did you say you're from?" I asked, looking up.

"Inverness," Lestrade repeated. "It's in …"

"Scotland," Jillian finished, after Lestrade had trailed off. She looked over at the British sergeant, but saw him looking at the dogs. Both were on their feet and both were staring at the phone on the desk. "What's with them? Zachary, any idea what they're doing?"

I looked at my dogs and held up my hands in a *who knows* gesture. Just like that, the phone started ringing.

Lestrade pointed at the dogs. "How did they …?"

"Don't ask," I interrupted, giving the DS a grin. "Hello? Yes, this is Zachary Anderson. What can I do for …? What's that? Yes, we're fine, thank you. No, we're both fine and we don't need anything. Thanks for checking. Yep. Bye. All right, sorry 'bout that. That was the front desk. They were just making sure everything is okay."

"Your dogs knew your phone was going to

ring without it making a sound?" Lestrade asked, amazed.

"If you're going to be hanging around us, you'd better get used to it," I told the DS. "These two dogs are amazing. True to their namesakes, they've solved all manner of crimes back home in the United States."

The DS couldn't hide his skepticism.

"Oh, sure, they have," Lestrade chuckled. "What did they solve? Missing bones?"

"The last bones they discovered," Jillian idly began, "they not only determined who they belonged to, but also that it was from a cold case which happened over fifty years ago. They've solved murders, located missing persons, and even found stolen property."

"Even when it came from a mysterious silver chest," I laughed, nodding.

Lestrade was suddenly staring at us, wide-eyed. "No! This is Sherlock and Watson, from the news?"

"They made the news over here?" I asked, impressed.

"If they found what I think they found, then yes, they did," Lestrade confirmed.

"I don't like pointing out that I've handled some super expensive jewelry," I explained, using a low tone of voice. "So, if I say silver puzzle box, then everyone who knows me will know what I'm talking about."

"I certainly know what you're talking about," Lestrade confessed. "Of course! That's why they wanted to assign a liaison. I should have known!"

"Care to share?" I asked.

"I can't expand on that, I'm afraid," Lestrade said, shaking his head. "Blimey, I can't believe I'm in the same room as Sherlock and Watson. This is amazing! Can I take your dogs' picture?"

Shaking my head, I stepped out of the way, followed closely by Jillian. While Lestrade took several snaps of the dogs, and presumably sent them off to people he knew, I picked up Joshua's file from where Lestrade had dropped it and looked at the name of the storage facility again. Cryptex Solutions. Well, a quick search online confirmed that it *is* a storage facility, only from what I could see, it was unlike any storage complex I had ever seen.

For starters, I could tell there was something up with this place when, unlike every storage facility I had seen, the only visible building was one small-ish structure that had several rows of parking spaces. Encircling this area was a very impressive metal and stone fence that had to be at least a dozen feet high. Also of note was the presence of a guard shack, which according to their website, was manned twenty-four hours a day, seven days a week.

If this was a storage facility, where were the storage units? Well, the answer was directly in front of me, if I would care to scroll a bit further down on the website: underground. Apparently, these people took their security seriously. There'd be no unauthorized entry into these units, believe me. What did all of that mean?

Easy. Cryptex Solutions respected their clients' privacy, no doubt about it. So, it begged the question, *what* was being stored in there? Clearly, it was something highly valuable, and more than likely, illegal as heck. Why else would they go to such trouble to make it practically impossible to access?

"You've gone quiet," Jillian observed. "Is everything all right?"

I handed her my phone. "I was just researching the storage facility Joshua was working on. See anything out of the ordinary?"

"The storage units are located underground?" Jillian asked, after glancing through the official website. "And the main access is protected by armed guards every hour of the day. It seems rather shady to me."

DS Lestrade held out a hand and waited for Jillian to hand him my phone. After reading through what the facility was offering, and how difficult it was to gain access after depositing items in the lockers, he started to nod.

"I've heard of these types of places. Maximum security, and so many fail safes in place that any attempt to illegally enter would typically result in the contents of the units being destroyed."

"Why in the world would anyone agree to have their stuff destroyed?" I wanted to know.

Jillian shrugged. "More than likely, the things being stored here? They shouldn't have them to begin with. The last thing anyone would want is to be caught with them in their possession."

"How is a place like this even legal?" I demanded.

Lestrade shrugged. "It's a gray area, to be sure. There's access through the main gate, provided you can make it past the guards, and I'm sure there is a nice, long list of dos and don'ts that Cryptex Solutions had to follow. The simple fact that they have been in business for nearly ten years tells me that they know what they're doing."

"Or," I added, holding up a finger, "that they have a fantastic legal team." A notion dawned on me, and it had me gasping for breath. I held up my phone and waggled it in front of Jillian and the DS. "That's where he found it."

Jillian looked at me. "That's where *who* found *what*?"

"The silver chest? Think about it. Is there any other place more secure than this one to hold something that doesn't belong to them? If Josh was researching this place, then this was more than likely how he learned of the chest's existence. Somehow, and I don't know how, he got his hands on it."

Jillian frowned. "Didn't you say the chest was shipped from Wales?"

"How far is Wales from here?" I asked Lestrade. "And, for curiosity's sake, which direction?"

Gary scratched his head. "Well, Cardiff is about two hundred forty kilometers to the west. Er, *that* way. It'll typically take about three hours to make a drive that far."

"Standard, dude," I groaned. "My mind doesn't think in metric terms."

Lestrade looked questioningly at Jillian.

"About one hundred fifty miles?" my fiancée guessed.

"That's fairly accurate," Lestrade admitted, giving Jillian a bow. "Very nicely done, madam."

Jillian's smile melted off her face as she stared at the young detective. That's one thing I've learned about Jillian. To hear the word madam suggests someone … I don't know, matronly? Nevertheless, it was a term of endearment my fiancée didn't care for in the slightest.

I started to smile, too, until my lovely significant other noticed and I got thumped in the gut. Briefly wondering if either of the dogs would come to my defense—which they've done in the past—I saw that no such demonstrations of chivalry were on the agenda for today. Both dogs continued to watch the proceedings from the bed.

"Don't say a word, Zachary."

I mimed zipping my lips closed. Our British friend, however, was at a loss.

"Did I miss something?"

"Nothing that bears repeating," Jillian said, shaking her head.

Giving both dogs a pat on the head, I sat down between them on the bed. "Okay, look. We know Josh is missing. Does your report say *when* he was reported missing?"

Lestrade held out his hand and indicated he wanted me to pass him the file. Once he had it, he quickly skimmed through several pages. "Here it is. Three days ago. He didn't report for work, and when we sent a constable to check on his whereabouts, we discovered his flat had been ransacked."

"Three days ago," I repeated. "That would mean he disappeared right after he sent you that message."

"What message was this?" Lestrade wanted to know.

Jillian retrieved her phone and showed the DS the message.

"Hmm. Remember the chest. That's the silver chest you were talking about earlier?"

Jillian nodded. "That's right. He sent it to Zachary, and when we were finally able to open it, well, you can imagine our surprise in finding something that had been reported stolen over a hundred years ago."

"Your dogs are amazing," Lestrade said, grinning. He ruffled Sherlock's fur before moving over to Watson. "I would love to know how two little dogs were able to solve a murder case, or how they're able to locate missing items."

"Oftentimes they're the same case," Jillian reminded me.

Nodding, I smiled at my fiancée. "Very true. Murders, missing property, locating missing fugitives, and ... let's see. What else?"

"They cracked the dognapping case."

I snapped my fingers. "That's right, they did."

"You two are local heroes, aren't you?" Lestrade praised. Both dogs, mind you, were panting contentedly and had their long pink tongues flopped out of their mouths. "The Queen will absolutely *love* meeting you two."

"Speaking of which," I said, "what do you know of that? We were invited to something called an audience. It wasn't until I looked it up online did I learn it was the Queen's way of sending out an invitation."

"Many people would love to be in your shoes," Lestrade told me. "And, I will say, the Queen does grant many audiences, but obviously, she can't grant audiences to everyone who requests it. So, to be granted an audience, without seeking one, is a high honor."

"You know more than you're letting on," Jillian said, smiling.

Lestrade grinned. "I'm sure I don't follow."

"Oh, yes you do," Jillian countered. "You know she's sent us the audience invitation. You know we didn't request it. You say you're here as a liaison for New Scotland Yard. I think that's just a cover. They sent you specifically, didn't they? They wanted you to watch us and keep us out of trouble."

Lestrade looked left, and then right, as though he thought he was being watched. When he knew he wasn't, he faced Jillian and bowed. "Let's keep that to ourselves, shall we? As far as New Scotland Yard is concerned, I'm DS Gary Lestrade."

"Is that even your real name?" I asked, dropping my voice to a whisper.

"Name, yes, title, no," Lestrade said, nodding. "And, for the record, that's the quickest anyone has ever outed me. Well done, Ms. Cooper."

"Why are you really here?" Jillian asked, in a hushed tone.

"The only thing I'm allowed to tell you, at this time, is that your brother was a valued asset of MI6, and that his disappearance is unacceptable. I've been tasked with helping you look into his disappearance."

"That means you're going to help us check out this storage facility?" I asked.

Lestrade nodded. "I am, yes."

"If the Queen liked my brother that much," Jillian began, "then why isn't she launching her own investigation into his disappearance?"

Lestrade fell silent as he returned Jillian's frank stare.

"Because, she *is*," I whispered. "The good Queen has brought *us* over here. She doesn't want a meeting. She wants to see if Sherlock and Watson can solve this case!"

Lestrade spread his hands in a helpless manner. "I can neither confirm nor deny that, I'm sorry. What I can tell you is that words of your dogs' deeds have reached her ears. As you may be aware, she is a huge fan of the breed. You lot are guests in our country. Consider this our way of keeping an eye on you."

"I think I'm okay with that," Jillian decided, as she looked over at me. "Very well. Where do we start?"

"Cryptex Solutions," I answered. "According to the file, that's the last project Josh was working on. After all, we're pretty sure that's where he found the chest."

"If that chest *did* come from this storage facility," Jillian began, "then ..."

"... what *else* might they have hidden away?" I finished, eliciting a nod from Jillian.

Lestrade nodded and pulled out his phone. "Leave the warrant to me. For the record, I think you're right. We all need to go see what's going on at Cryptex Solutions."

THREE

W ell, that didn't go quite the way I had hoped," I grumbled, as the three of us, five if you included the dogs, returned to our hotel after a very unsuccessful attempt to gain entry to Cryptex Solutions. "I can only assume the people who use that place want to remain anonymous and wield more power than we do."

"It would seem they have some very influential friends," Lestrade admitted. "Fear not. I'm sure we'll be able to get that warrant, only it's going to take longer than we want."

"What should we do in the meantime?" Jillian asked, as we entered the front lobby of our hotel.

Sherlock and Watson perked up as they passed the front desk. Both corgis paused to look at the girl behind the counter. The young clerk took one look at my two dogs and practically squealed with delight.

"Oh, look at your dogs! They're adorable! May I pet them?"

"Well, that depends," I said, giving the girl a mock-serious smile. "If you're willing to make two friends for life, then go right ahead."

We watched as the girl hurried around the counter and dropped down into a sitting position right there on the floor. She started making cooing noises at the dogs, which resulted in Watson going belly-up. Sherlock elected to sit next to his packmate and watch the hotel clerk, as though he didn't quite trust her.

"What's he looking at?" Jillian whispered in my ear. Thankfully, we were standing far enough away from the frolicking dogs that we weren't overheard. "You'd think he suspects something."

I shook my head. "I don't know. He started watching her the moment we walked through the door. The girl seems nice enough."

The desk phone started ringing. The girl quickly rose to her feet and returned to the counter. From the sounds of the conversation we could hear, it would appear that there was someone who wanted to make a reservation on the other end of the line. Once done, the girl reached for something we couldn't see and returned to her position on the floor.

This time, she produced two doggie biscuits and held one out to each of the dogs. Watson was on her feet in a flash. She took her treat and re-treated a few steps to enjoy it. Sherlock studied the hand holding the treat and cocked his head, as though he couldn't figure out what he was seeing. Curious, I leaned around Jillian and saw Sherlock sniff the girl's hand. Maybe he wasn't sure about someone who chose to wear a ring on every single finger?

Sherlock chose that time to look over at me, as if asking permission, only when I nodded, he continued to stare at me. Sighing, I pulled my phone out, taking a picture just as he snatched the treat from the girl's hand. The girl returned to her feet as Sherlock started crunching through his goodie.

Dogs.

As I watched the girl return to her position behind the front desk, a thought occurred. We might not be able to check out Cryptex Solutions—yet— but we may be able to take a look at something else that could be vitally important. Especially since we have Dog Wonder and his faithful sidekick with us.

"Umm, excuse me? Allyson, is it? Hey, is there any way we could take a look at a room a friend of ours was staying in?"

Jillian's head lifted. "Oh, good one, Zachary."

"Which room would that be?" Allyson inquired.

"Whichever room First Sergeant Joshua Cooper stayed in," I answered, correctly remembering my brother-in-law's military title.

Allyson tapped several commands on her keyboard and waited for the computer to respond. When it apparently didn't give her the answer she expected, she frowned and looked up at me.

"I don't have anyone by that name staying with us right now."

"That's because he's not here at the moment," I explained.

"Oh. In that case, when was he here?"

I looked at Lestrade. "Does that file say when he checked in?"

Lestrade already had the file open and was skimming through a few pages. "Seven days ago."

There was more tapping on the keyboard. "Ah, here we are. One Josh Cooper checked in one week ago. The cleaners have already seen to the room, so there won't be anything to find in there, I'm sorry to report."

"Has it been occupied by anyone else?" I asked.

"The room is vacant," Allyson told me, "and has been that way since Mr. Cooper vacated the room."

"Did he?" I asked.

"Did *who* do *what*?" Lestrade asked, puzzled.

"Did Joshua check out from his room?" I asked.

Lestrade shook his head. "No. When he didn't report for work, we investigated and saw that he hadn't been back to his room for a few days. That's when we conducted our own investigation and gave permission for the room to be cleaned."

"I should've known you guys would've done your own investigation. So, can I ask if anything was found?"

Lestrade shrugged. "Nothing of importance. If I didn't know any better, I'd say Mr. Cooper cleaned up after himself."

"Did he take his things with him?" Jillian asked.

"No suitcases were found in the room," Lestrade reported. "No personal effects, clothes, or any type of sundries were found, other than what the hotel provides."

"So, there really isn't any need to look," Allyson decided, giving us a sad smile.

"May we still look?" Lestrade asked, as he flashed his ID to confirm we weren't some hooligans off the street.

"Oh, of course. Let me program you a key. Here you go. Room #547. It's on the ..."

"... fifth floor?" I interrupted, offering the girl a smile.

"Exactly. The elevators are just through there."

"There's no need to tell us where the elevators are," I sighed, as we walked down a short hall, which curved to the right. "After all, we *are* currently staying here."

"She probably doesn't know that," Jillian said, coming to Allyson's defense.

"Yeah, yeah. All right, here we are: fifth floor. According to the sign, we need to head to the left. Yep, that's it. Who's got the card?"

"I do," Lestrade announced, as he held it against the door's sensor. "After you."

The room was an exact replica of our own. The bed was against the left wall, the desk was there, with the multi-line phone, and the bathroom was behind us, just as we came in the room. Lestrade looked at me and indicated I should take the lead. Well, that was easy enough to do.

I dropped the dogs' leashes.

"If there's anything to be found in this room," I said, "then these two will be able to find it. They are the absolute *best* at finding clues. Granted, they might not make too much sense to us *now*, but it will at some point. So, guys? Do your thing. Where are you two going to look first? Maybe under the bed? Maybe in the closet? Or … I don't care where you look, but just look, all right?"

Sherlock glanced briefly at me, looked left, and then right. His furry rear sank down on the carpeted floor and then he slowly lowered himself into a down position.

"What are you doing? Come on, pal. Don't make a liar out of me. Isn't there anything in here you want to look at?"

Watson lowered herself into a down position as well. As one, both corgis stared at me and watched me intently. If I didn't know any better, I'd say they were humoring me by being in here, as though I was the one who needed to do the investigating. "What about you, Watson? Would you care to look around?"

I was ignored.

"They don't want to look around?" Lestrade said, chagrined. "And here I was hoping that they …"

"Hold up," Jillian interrupted. "Zachary, they've done this before."

I turned to look at the dogs. That was true. The only reason they *wouldn't* want to do any investigating was if there simply was nothing to investigate. Didn't Allyson tell us that the housekeepers had already cleaned the room?

"There's nothing here to find," I decided. "That's why they're not interested."

"And how would you know if they *were* interested?" Lestrade inquired.

"Well, usually the dogs would pull like crazy on their leashes," I explained. "They'd lead me to whatever had caught their attention and would literally wait there, refusing to be budged, until I took a picture of the offending item."

"And that's about when they'd both sit down," Jillian added.

"You're kidding," Lestrade scoffed.

"He isn't," Jillian confirmed. "But, I will say that, most of the time, no one has any clue as to what the corgis are looking at."

"It never makes sense at first," I added. "Eventually, I'll gather some friends, go to dinner, and together we'll review the pictures I've taken."

"And that's when you figure out what the dogs were looking at?" Lestrade guessed.

Jillian laughed. "Not at all. The pictures usually don't make sense until the case has been solved."

Lestrade held up a hand. "So, did you take a picture of our friend Allyson?"

I looked up. "What was that?"

"Sherlock and Watson were staring at the girl

at the counter," Lestrade recalled. "Did you end up taking a picture of her?"

I held up my phone. "As a matter of fact, I did."

"Were they sitting?"

"Uh, I think so?"

Lestrade nodded. "Interesting. All right, if your dogs aren't going to investigate, then, as you say, there's nothing here to find. Let's head out, shall we?"

"Where to next?" I asked, as I headed for the door, resulting in both corgis leaping to their feet.

Lestrade grinned. "Well, I was thinking we should check out the one thing your dogs *did* seem to be interested in."

I looked at Jillian, who immediately pointed straight down. Uncertain of what she meant, I looked down at the shag brown carpet. "Umm ..."

"The front desk," Jillian explaining, which earned her a nod from Lestrade. "Sherlock and Watson fixated on the front desk."

"That's only because the girl was nice," I protested.

"And what about the fact that Allyson wasn't here when we first checked in?" Jillian recalled. "It was someone completely different."

I felt like snapping my fingers. The dogs *did* zero in on the desk. I just assumed they were wanting more attention from passing onlookers.

"Did they now?" Lestrade said. "Well, now I'm doubly curious."

"Fine. Sherlock? Watson? Lead the way, would

you? Back downstairs."

Both dogs were instantly on their feet and heading back to the elevators. The moment the elevator doors opened, however, both dogs came to an immediate stop. There, on the opposite wall from the elevators, was a simple blue sign describing the hours the hotel's indoor pool was open. Both dogs sat, prompting us humans to stare at the sign as though it was printed in another language.

"Why are they staring at this?" Lestrade wanted to know.

I shrugged and pulled out my phone. "No clue. Watch this. As soon as I take the picture, which is what they want me to do, then they'll be back on their feet and on their way."

"No way," Lestrade laughed.

I snapped a photo, the dogs immediately rose to their feet, and sure enough, we were off.

"I had no idea dogs could be so smart."

"Just these two," Jillian warned. "I had a dog growing up that was the sweetest thing ever, but was definitely a few sandwiches short of a picnic."

The minute we returned to the lobby, I was forcefully pulled to the front desk by my team of Clydesdales and once more, we were standing before the check-in clerk. This time, however, Allyson was not there.

"Good day to you all," the middle-aged man behind the counter said, as he looked over at us and smiled. Hearing one of the dogs shake a collar, he leaned over the counter and looked down. "Ah, these must be the two corgis I've heard so much about. Good day to you, too, my fine fellows. So, how can I help you?"

I produced the room card and slid it across the counter. "We'd like to return this, and please extend our thanks to Allyson."

Without missing a beat, or even inquiring which room the card opened, the male clerk nodded and dropped the card into a box of what I assumed was used room keys. When he looked back up at me, he raised an eyebrow, in proper Vulcan fashion.

"Will there be anything else?"

I turned to my companions. "I have no idea what we're looking for."

My fiancée came to my rescue.

"Do you have a lost and found here?"

The male clerk nodded. "As a matter of fact, we do, yes. Have you lost an item?"

"We just came from room #547. By any chance, did the previous occupant leave anything behind?"

"I could only disclose that if you were next of kin."

Jillian nodded and reached for her purse. Producing her identification, she held it for the clerk to see.

"My name is Jillian Cooper. My brother, Joshua Cooper, was formerly in that room, and has since disappeared. I'm just checking to see if he might have left anything behind."

As if this was the most ordinary of requests, the

clerk nodded once. "Of course. Just a moment, and I will check."

"What are the chances?" I asked.

"Based on what you've told me about your dogs," Lestrade said, looking down at Sherlock and Watson, "I'd say better than average. I have to admit I'm intrigued. Look at them! They're staring at the counter as though they expect … that is, they think … that maybe Her Majesty the Queen is going to make an appearance?"

Five minutes later, the clerk was back. I felt my heart race as I noticed he was carrying something, which he handed to Jillian.

"For room #547, this is all we had, I'm afraid," the clerk said. "We hereby return it to its rightful owner."

"And you're certain this didn't belong to a previous occupant of the room?" Lestrade inquired.

The clerk nodded. "Housekeeping tells me this was recovered only a few days ago."

"Then it definitely belonged to my brother," Jillian said, growing excited. "Can you tell me where it was found?"

"It was found in room #547," the clerk repeated.

"No, I mean, where in the room was it found?" Jillian specified.

"Oh, my apologies. Let me ask." The clerk reached for the phone, punched one of the many buttons on the console, and waited a few moments. "Brigitte? It's me again. About that recovered notebook, can you tell me *where* it was found in the room? The owner's sister is here, and she was inquiring about the method in which it was found. Oh, it was? Did you look under ... I see. Very well, I'll pass along the information. Thank you, Brigitte." The handset was replaced and the clerk motioned Jillian over. "That notebook? Well, apparently, it was taped under the desk. I was informed that, when vacuuming, the desk was nudged, and the notebook dropped to the floor. Looking under the desk revealed several pieces of duct tape."

"Don't all rooms come with those little locking safes?" I asked.

The clerk nodded. "They do, and that particular room had one, in the closet. Why this wasn't locked away remains unclear."

"That's easy," Lestrade said. "Everyone knows hotels provide safes in all their rooms. If you want to hide something, you wouldn't make it blatantly obvious, would you?"

Jillian thanked the clerk and then made for the front entrance, beckoning us to follow her.

"So, did you find something?" I asked, edging close.

"Apparently, this was something he didn't want anyone to find."

"What is it?" Lestrade asked. "Another notebook?"

She held up the simple spiral-bound notebook, the kind most schoolkids use, flipped it open, and immediately frowned: the first few pages were blank.

"What's the matter?" I asked, as I sidled close to peer over her shoulder. "Oh. There's nothing there. That stinks."

"Can you tell if it belonged to your brother?" Lestrade wanted to know.

Jillian shrugged. "It's hard to say. I know he's used notebooks like this one, but it doesn't mean this one is his. For all we know, this one could've belonged to a previous occupant of the room."

Jillian made a move to hand the notebook back when I noticed the dogs. Both were absolutely fixated on that notebook. Placing a hand on Jillian's shoulder, I took the item found in Josh's room and lifted it high in the air.

The dogs tracked the notebook.

I moved it left, then right. Up, and then down. No matter where I moved it, the dogs stared at it, as though this notebook had been used as a coaster for a honey-baked ham.

Jillian stared at the corgis for a few moments before taking back the notebook. "That seals it. There *must* be something here we're missing, but what?"

I watched my fiancée open the notebook for a second time, to start flipping through the pages, when I noticed the lower right corner. If I wasn't mistaken, I could see that one of the pages looked as though it was dog-eared.

"I think you're looking for that."

Jillian looked up. "What's that? What did you

say?"

Lestrade noticed and he wordlessly pointed at the notebook.

"Most people will fold a corner back in a magazine, or notebook, in order to bookmark a page."

Jillian nodded, and gave me a look which suggested she couldn't believe I had to explain this to her.

"Lower right corner. I think I see a dog-eared page."

Holding the notebook up, Jillian's eyes widened as she spotted the crimped paper. "Well, well, what have we here?"

"What is it?" I asked, crowding close.

"Zachary, it's Joshua's writing! I'd recognize it anywhere!"

"What does it say?" Lestrade asked.

"It's just some notes. There are references to a library, and a museum. It just doesn't say which ones. Oh, wait. Here's something. Does the Magnificent Cullinan mean anything to anyone?"

Lestrade fell silent and stared at Jillian for a few moments before stepping closer to see for himself what was written. He noticed Jillian had said exactly what was written, grunted once, and leaned back. After a few moments, he shook his head.

"Of all the things I thought could have been written inside that notebook, *that* was nowhere to be found."

"The Magnificent Cullinan?" Jillian repeated,

reading the words again. "Who is it?"

"You mean, *what* is it, of course. The Magnificent Cullinan is the largest diamond that has ever been found. Why your brother would be researching that is beyond me, I'm afraid."

Jillian pulled out her phone and did an online search.

"The Magnificent Cullinan," Jillian intoned, as she began to read, "was discovered in South Africa in 1905. Let's see, it looks like it was named after the chairman of the mining company, one Thomas Cullinan. It says here that, in its raw, uncut state, the stone weighed in at over 3,100 carats."

Wow! Now *that* was a big diamond! What in the world was Joshua doing investigating it? After all, it wasn't stolen, was it?

"Can we double check that diamond is where it's supposed to be?" I asked, as I turned to Lestrade.

Our New Scotland Yard liaison nodded, pulled out his cell, and hurried off. Thankfully, he must have received good news because he was back in less than twenty seconds.

"It's fine. The Tower guards just did a walk-through a few moments ago."

Jillian and I looked at each other. "The Tower guards?"

Lestrade nodded. "Well, that diamond is housed with the crown jewels. You didn't know that?"

Both Jillian and myself shook our heads.

"Needless to say, the diamond is fine. In fact, the Magnificent Cullinan, and all the diamonds that were cut from it, are still under lock and key. I was assured they were just fine."

"How many diamonds was it cut down to?" I asked, curious.

"Every British school child knows this," Lestrade said, grinning. "The Magnificent Cullinan was cut into nine major stones and, count 'em, ninety-six smaller stones."

"That's amazing," Jillian exclaimed.

Hearing a collar rattle, I glanced down at the dogs, fully expecting to see them in reclining positions. After all, they had done their job and alerted us to the presence of the notebook, and the fact that there was something useful inside. Typically, after that happens, Sherlock and Watson will lose interest in the item. That is, if there isn't anything else to learn from it. What were the corgis doing?

Staring, transfixed, at the notebook.

"May I see that?" I inquired.

Jillian handed me the notebook and, while she and Lestrade chatted about this magnificent what's-it-called diamond, I flipped through the pages. There was clearly something about this notebook that the dogs wanted us to see.

"What is it, guys? There's nothing else in here, I assure you."

Sherlock snorted once and continued to stare at me.

I held the notebook down low. "See for yourself.

There's nothing here. Hey, what are you doing?"

Sherlock had nudged the notebook out of my hand. It clattered to the floor and was nosed a few times by both dogs. Grumbling, I retrieved the book and straightened. Fine. We were all clueless nitwits who couldn't find the ...

I trailed off as I flipped the page with the notes about the diamond. There, on the flip-side of the page was the answer. A second line of notes had been scribbled out, and this time, it was in the form of some type of equation.

$$8(4((5*2) - 3) + 17/2)) + ((8/2 * 8) + 11/5))$$

"What do you have there?" Lestrade asked, as he glanced at the notebook. A frown immediately appeared on his face. "What's this? A math problem? Oh, I hate math. You two are on your own."

"Joshua," Jillian whispered, as she stared at the equation. "Only he would concoct something like this."

"Your brother routinely created math problems for you?" I asked.

"Not exactly like this, but this was always his way. He was always coming up with secret ways to tell me things."

"And you believe he's trying to say something with that bunch of junk?" Lestrade asked.

Jillian nodded and fished through her purse until she pulled out a pen. Then, she calmly walked over to several recliners in the hotel's lobby and sat down. "I say we solve the equation and see if I'm right about it."

Lestrade stared at the long string of numbers and symbols and shook his head. "I wasn't kidding before, when I stated that equation looked like junk."

"You don't like math?" Jillian asked, as she settled herself into the recliner.

"I *hate* math," Lestrade confirmed. "You're on your own, I'm afraid. What about you, Zachary? Do you think you could solve it?"

Studying the long equation, I eventually nodded. "I'd have to refresh my memory about the order of equations, but yeah, it's just a matter of tackling that thing in the right order."

"Huh?" Lestrade stammered.

Jillian tapped the page. "Do you see this, here? I'm talking about this part of the left side of the equation. These parentheses mean we're essentially going to be adding one number to another."

"How do you figure?" Lestrade asked, bewildered. "Look at all those numbers. How do you get just two?"

"You have to look at the parentheses. They're handled first. This four? You multiply it by the results of this section. But, before you can do that, you have to solve the section first. There's an eight, and it has to be multiplied by the results of *this* section. And this one? It's just this times this, and then subtract that. Take that number and add it to this. What do you get?"

"A headache," Lestrade groaned.

"I'm serious, detective. What do you get? Zachary?"

"Fifteen and a half," I answered.

Jillian nodded. "Precisely."

"Now, wait a minute," Lestrade protested. "How in the bloody hell did you come up with that? I may have hated math, but I thought I was better at it than that."

"What did you come up with?" Jillian asked.

"Twelve."

"Twelve?" Jillian and I echoed.

"Well, yeah. Those two give you ten. Subtract out the three and you get seven."

"With you so far," I said.

"Right. Take that seven and add it to the seventeen there, and then divide by two. What do you get?"

"The wrong answer," Jillian observed, giving the DS a smile. "You have to look at the order in which it is supposed to be solved. Take that seven and then add it to this one."

"I did that," Lestrade insisted.

"But, you have to solve this 17/2 part first. What does it work out to be?"

"Oh. Um … give me a sec. Eight. Eight and a half. Ah, I get it. That's how you came up with fifteen and a half?"

Jillian nodded. "Exactly. Take that number and multiply it by eight. What do you get?"

I had to pull out my phone and activate the calculator app.

"One hundred twenty-four."

Jillian added the answer to her paper.

"Now, take *that* number and multiply it by four."

"One twenty-four and one twenty-four is two forty-eight," I mumbled. "Double that and you get four hundred ninety-six."

"And you can do that in your head?" Lestrade complained.

I shrugged. "I've always been able to do the easy stuff in my head. What can I say? I liked math in school."

"So, is that the answer?" Lestrade asked. "Four hundred ninety-six?"

Jillian shook her head. "No, that's the first part of this equation. This part here. The second? It's much easier. The first part of this section? Eight divided by two is four, and then multiply it by eight. That's thirty-two. Add that to this fraction, which is 11/5, also known as 2.2, and you get ... altogether now ... 34.2."

Closing my eyes, I pictured the numbers in my head. "So, our answer would be the sum of four hundred ninety-six and 34.2, which gives us ... well, that's a weird number. Why would he write an equation to come up with *that* number?"

"What's the answer?" Lestrade asked, intrigued. "What did you get?"

I looked at Jillian. "The number I got was five hundred thirty point two."

There was a gasp of surprise, but oddly enough,

it didn't come from Jillian. Together, my fiancée and I looked at our British friend.

"Does that mean something to you?" I asked.

In response, Lestrade whipped out his phone and started tapping something out on the screen. Was he sending a text? Maybe looking up an answer to a question? A few moments later, Lestrade showed us his phone's display. On it was a big, fancy jewel.

"We're looking at a diamond," I said. "What about it?"

Lestrade tapped the phone. "This particular gemstone is one of the six stones that was cut from the Cullinan stone. It's actually part of the Crown Jewels."

"What does that particular diamond have to do with anything?" Jillian asked.

"Because," Lestrade explained, "this particular stone is *exactly* 530.2 carats in size. For whatever the reason, your brother was researching the Cullinan diamond. Or, more specifically, he wanted to draw attention to the Crown Jewels!"

FOUR

I've always wanted to do this. You've told me that you haven't been here before, either. I just wish we could be here under better circumstances. I think we'd enjoy it more."

I took my fiancée's hand tightly in my own and gave it a reassuring squeeze. "I know what you mean. But, look on the bright side."

Jillian gave me a worried look. "And what would that be?"

"We're going to experience it for the first time together. That's worth mentioning, isn't it?"

It was the following day, just before ten in the morning. That is to say, my phone is insisting that it's ten, but to me, it still felt like it was two in the morning, which is what time it'd be back in Pomme Valley. Jillian was faring better than I was, even though I kept catching her yawning when she thought no one was watching. Sherlock and Watson? They appeared to be unfazed by the number of time zones between here and home. They were both trotting ahead of us, as though they were royalty and we humans were the lowly peasants.

The skies were dark, the ground was wet, and the temp was a very respectable seventy-two. Armed with umbrellas, and me wearing a backpack with just about every conceivable item a tourist would need, especially for one with dogs, we stopped at a decent viewpoint of the Thames and snapped a selfie. Seeing how the drizzle had stopped—for the time being—we both shoved our umbrellas into my pack.

As for the dogs? Let's just say I had an emergency towel in the pack. Being built so low to the ground, any attempt for a corgi to walk over wet ground would inevitably result in wet underbellies. In this case, I swear Sherlock was angling for the larger puddles. He'd see one coming, and I'd feel the leashes lean in that direction, and I'd groan with dismay.

"We'll have to clean them off when we get back to the room."

Directly before us was a large plaza, announcing we had arrived in the right spot. Just like any amusement park, there was a front entrance, where tourists could purchase an admission ticket. A quick glance around revealed this particular spot also doubled as a gift shop. In fact, I had just spotted something that I wanted to purchase for Jillian.

"Jillian? Take Sherlock's leash, would you? I'll

handle this."

"Thank you, Zachary."

Less than five minutes later, with my recent purchases stuffed into the dogs' backpack, I
pointed at the little café. "Before we check out the
jewels, did you want to get a bite to eat?" I asked.

Jillian nodded. "That's a good idea. Hmm, I
think I'll use the restroom first. Would you hold on
to the dogs for me?" She handed over both leashes.

"Absolutely."

I watched Jillian head toward a public restroom
and slowly looked around. If someone would've
told me that, in less than a year, I'd not only be
engaged to be married, but would be making a trip
across the seas to look for a missing cryptologist,
then I would have definitely called them a nutjob.
On top of which, we were also going to have to
carve out time to meet with the Queen.

That one still made me shake my head. The
Queen of England. We're here to meet up with the
Queen, so she can meet Sherlock and Watson. Holy
crap on a cracker. There was an opener for any so-
cial occasion, let me tell you.

Just then, I noticed Jillian exiting the restroom
with a look of bewilderment on her face.

"What's the matter?" I asked, growing cautious.
"If you tell me you found a hidden message from
Joshua, then I'm personally checking myself into a
funny farm."

Jillian shook her lovely head. "Er, no. It's, um,
well ..."

Was she tongue-tied? What in the world happened in that restroom? I mean, she didn't look distraught, but she did appear rather flummoxed.

"Just tell me what the problem is," I implored.

"I need fifty pence."

"Huh?"

"I need a fifty pence coin."

"What—?"

Jillian turned to look back at the restroom. "The room with the stalls? They're locked. In order to use one, you have to pay them fifty pence. By chance, do you have a fifty pence coin?"

"I was given some change when I bought this," I said, holding up the bag with Jillian's souvenir Tower of London guide. "Let me see what I have. Hey, look at this one. It's a one-pound coin. Would that work?"

Jillian nodded. "According to the instructional sticker on the wall, it'll work. Thank you, Zachary."

Paying to use the restrooms. What a concept. Then again, converting restrooms into pay-as-you-go (pun intended) facilities would be a wonderful way to help pay for the upkeep and offset any maintenance costs. Maybe I should bring it up to the …

Jillian emerged from the restroom. I knew right away that it was too soon of a turn-around time, so something must have happened, and based on the frown she was wearing, it wasn't good.

"Umm, is everything all right?" I asked.

"I couldn't go. It *ate* my money."

Several seconds of silence passed as I attempted to place what Jillian had said into context. She wanted to use the facilities, and it had denied her? *And* took her money? Were we being filmed?

"Umm ..."

"Forget about it. I see a nice little restaurant over there, with outdoor seating. We can order some lunch and I'll just use their facilities."

Doing a remarkable job of holding my face in neutral, I agreed.

Twenty minutes later, we were enjoying our lunch. Well, at least, I was *trying* to. I learned something about myself that day: I don't like English bacon. I had just assumed—erroneously—that English bacon was close enough to its American equivalent that it shouldn't have posed a problem.

Wrong.

Jillian explained later that bacon in the UK, typically called *rashers*, is thicker and chewier than bacon served in the United States. Also, English bacon is usually served in round circles, much like a slice of meat from your neighborhood deli. American bacon? Crispy and smoked, and originates from pork belly. English bacon? Not smoked, and cut from the loin on the pig's back, where the meat is much leaner. Since I am a huge admirer of pork, and practically all its forms, I was surprised to learn I wasn't a fan of this variety. It *had* to be the absence of smoke. Nevertheless, the foreign bacon was still welcomed on my hamburger and fries. Er, chips. I guess I should use the correct term the locals use.

I produced a bowl from my pack and gave the dogs some water. The two corgis then settled to the ground and were content to watch the people passing by. I'd also like to point out that nearly everyone who did pass us by stopped long enough to offer a compliment to the dogs.

Corgis are truly loved in this country, no doubt about it.

With tickets in hand, and Jillian holding her gift with her free hand, we entered what reminded me of a castle's courtyard. Multi-story crenellated stone walls, interspersed with both square and round towers every twenty feet or so, met our eyes. Information kiosks were everywhere, and they even included *You are here* maps on the opposite side. Studying the layout, I couldn't help but notice the abundance of small gift shop stalls and food carts. This place truly did remind me of an amusement park.

Detecting movement in my peripheral vision, I turned to watch one of the Queen's foot soldiers, dressed in the traditional red tunic and bearskin hat, slowly march by, stepping high with each step. I'd like to say that, to me, and my untrained eyes, it looked a little silly. However, one look at the young soldier's impassive face suggested he took his responsibilities very seriously. Yes, he was armed, and yes, that weapon was probably real. No wonder so many people tried to make these impeccably dressed guards break rank. They acted as if they were in their own little world. Personally, I think you don't want to aggravate someone holding a high-powered weapon.

"How soon before we're due to meet Lestrade?" I asked.

"About ten minutes. We should probably head over there. That seems to be the entrance to the crown jewels."

As we stepped inside the darkened hall, we passed a sign that prohibited flash photography and video recording. That was a bummer. I had been hoping to take a few pictures of this Cullinan diamond, seeing how Jillian's brother was so fascinated by it.

We nodded at the uniformed staff member collecting tickets. He smiled at the corgis and tipped his hat as we passed. I watched Jillian pull out her souvenir guidebook as we slowly wandered along the length of the nearest display case. Inside was something so shiny and sparkly that the first thing I thought of was costume jewelry. However, every single sign I passed assured me that these jewels were all real.

Inside the case was a bejeweled crown resting on a small felt-lined stand. I could also see a sceptre or two, and even something that looked like a solid gold baseball.

"Ah, there you are," a voice announced.

Turning, we saw Detective Sergeant Gary Lestrade approach. Today, he had on a dark green, long-sleeved business shirt, paired with khakis.

The DS smiled warmly at Jillian before nodding his head at me.

"Magnificent, aren't they?" Lestrade praised, as he turned to look at the display we had just been admiring.

I looked inside the case at the gold and purple crown, adorned with jewels so big that my brain balked when I tried guessing their value, and shook my head.

"Those jewels are so big that they look fake. I know what the sign says, but I want your honest answer: are those things all real?"

"As real as you and me," Lestrade confirmed.

"And people wear that? It looks … uncomfortable."

Lestrade chuckled. "Oh, it is. All of the gold in that crown is the reason it weighs 2.23 kg."

"And what is that in pounds?" I asked.

Lestrade sighed. "Nearly five, I believe."

"That doesn't seem so bad," I decided.

"That is St. Edward's Crown," Lestrade explained. "It replaced the original crown in 1649. What's fascinating is that, up until the early twentieth century, that crown contained hired gems."

"Hired gems?" Jillian repeated, puzzled.

"Yes, er, that means the gems were borrowed for special occasions, and when the ceremony was over, the gems were returned. Well, in 1911, permanent stones were added, thus becoming what you're looking at today."

"It's beautiful," Jillian breathed. "And, for the

record, I would never want to carry around five pounds on my head. Talk about giving yourself a headache."

"Oh, please," Lestrade scoffed. "You all know how old our Queen is, don't you? She wore it and didn't have any problems."

"She was also coronated in 1953," Jillian responded, without missing a beat. "That would make her, what, twenty-five?"

Lestrade nodded. "You know your history."

"What's with the fancy baseball?" I asked, as I pointed at the golden sphere sitting inside the display case, next to the crown.

"That's the Sovereign's Orb," Lestrade explained. "It was also put into use starting in 1661. Baseball, indeed. Have you seen many baseballs encrusted with as many gemstones as that?"

"Well, no."

"Do you see the cross on top of it?"

Jillian and I both nodded.

"That cross symbolizes the Christian world."

Neither of us were religious, so that particular comment garnered a *hmm* from Jillian and a *huh* from me.

"What do you do with it?" I asked. "What's its purpose?"

"That orb is placed into the new monarch's right hand," Lestrade said. Moments later, he shrugged. "As far as I'm aware, its only purpose is symbolic."

"Links the church and the crown together," I

decided.

"Precisely. Now, if you'll look over here, I think you'll find this interesting."

"What is it?" Jillian asked.

Sherlock and Watson decided at that exact moment that whatever was in the case, well, they wanted it. They managed to rear up on their hind legs and deposit several of their doggie-based nose art creations on the glass. Pulling them sharply away from the long display case, the corgis promptly turned into their draft horse personas and tried to pull me around to the opposite side of the case.

"I can see it just fine from here, guys. Thanks."

Sure enough, I was ignored. Prior to owning these two, I never would have imagined two dogs, and ones with little, squat legs at that, could be so freakishly strong. I'm surprised there weren't gouges on the cement floor from where I dug in my heels to where I was pulled.

"Fine. You got me over here. What about it? It's just the flip side of the same thing. Now, would you knock it off?"

Lestrade flashed me a patient smile before ticking off a few facts about the Sovereign's Sceptre, which is what we were now staring at.

"This sceptre has been used in every coronation since Charles II in 1661."

"There's that year again," I said. "1661. Sounds like all kinds of stuff happened that year."

Jillian pointed at the sceptre's head. "So, can we

assume that the huge jewel right there is the Cullinan diamond Joshua was researching?"

"Yes and no," Lestrade said. "Yes, this is the gem your brother was referring to when he created that mathematical equation. No, this isn't technically the Cullinan diamond. It's referred to as the Star of Africa, or the Cullinan I."

"I see. It's one of the six cut from the source stone," Jillian said, nodding. "Well, what's so spectacular about it? Aside from being absolutely gorgeous, that is."

"That sucker is huge," I admitted, as I leaned over the case to stare down at it from above. "I'm telling you, those jewels are so fancy-looking that they *have* to be fake."

"They're not," Lestrade insisted.

"Yeah, I know," I said. "It's just so crazy knowing those jewels are the real thing. All right, moving on. That funky equation? The one Joshua did? He was making it clear that he was researching this particular diamond. My question is, why? And, knowing what we know, what can we do about it? I can pretty much guarantee you that *this* is as close as we're going to get to it."

Jillian appeared by my side and, together, we stared at the huge diamond.

"What do we do, Zachary?"

Right on cue, as though they had been waiting for that very question to be asked, I felt twin tugs on the leashes. Both corgis were threatening to rear up again. I felt a brief flash of anger, and then a really big flash of stupidity. The dogs were trying to tell me something! Perhaps I should be paying attention?

"What is it, guys?" I asked, lowering my voice to a whisper. "You two clearly want me to look at this case. Well, I'm looking. We all are. What is it you want to show us?"

Sherlock reared up on his hind legs and touched the underside with his nose. Since the glass display case was, in essence, sitting on its own pedestal, and it was smaller than the case, there was a significant overlap on all four sides. Sherlock and Watson wanted me to check out the undersides? How? Why? I suddenly flashed back to the hotel room, and the manner in which Joshua had been able to hide the notebook. Could it be that simple? A quick check of the display case would let me know one way or the other. The problem was, performing this inspection was going to make me look suspicious as heck. I'd be lucky if I wasn't discovered and escorted out of here.

"Is anyone watching?"

"Zachary Michael, what are you doing?" Jillian demanded, using a horrified whisper.

"I'm not going to do anything. I have a hunch, and I'm checking it out, all right? Now, let me know if anyone comes in."

"You're a police officer," I heard Jillian say to Lestrade. "Shouldn't you be stopping him?"

"If he damages anything in here, then I'll personally arrest him," Lestrade responded.

"Thanks, guys," I scoffed, as I started skimming my hands along the underside of the glass display case. Well, what I could reach, anyway. "I'm not doing anything bad. I'm just … hello, what do we have here?"

Jillian appeared on my right at the same time Lestrade materialized on my left.

"Did you find something?" Jillian asked.

While running my hand along the underside of the case, I had come across something that was sticking to the bottom of the case, held in place by a large piece of tape. I was in the process of scraping a corner of the tape back, so I could peel it off the display case, when we all heard footsteps. Giving the tape a rather violent jerk, I stuffed everything I had managed to grab into my pocket and motioned for everyone to follow me to the next display.

"What is it?" Lestrade whispered. "What'd you find?"

"Not here," I whispered back. "Not yet. I need to make certain we aren't being followed, or that no one suspects anything." Then, in a much louder voice … "So, what's in this one? Anything noteworthy?"

"Anything noteworthy?" Lestrade asked, incredulous. Then again, I could tell he was warming up to the game I was now playing. "You Americans. Everything in this room is priceless beyond compare, and is steeped in our country's history. Take this piece, for example."

Stepping up to the case, I gazed inside.

"So, it's another purple hat. Big whoop."

"It's a crown, you ninny," Lestrade scoffed, pretending to be insulted. "It's the Imperial State Crown. It contains some of the most historic gems in the entire collection."

I waved a dismissive hand. "Fine. Let's hear it."

Jillian clutched my hand in hers and stifled a giggle. The corgis, I'd like to add, were now staring at me. Or, more specifically, what was in my pocket. It was definitely encouraging.

"The Imperial State Crown," Lestrade began, "is worn by the monarch after leaving Westminster Abbey. Do you see the large ruby set into the cross?"

"Looks fake," I drawled.

"I know you're faking," Lestrade murmured, "but you'd better be careful, Yank."

I snorted with laughter.

"That ruby isn't a ruby. It's a spinel, and has a name."

"I'm all ears," I told our British friend.

"It's called The Black Prince's Ruby. Legend has it this is the same stone that was once owned by Pedro the Cruel, King of Castile."

Jillian sighed. "Let me guess. He was called the Black Prince?"

Lestrade nodded. "No. That title belongs to Edward of Wales. Pedro gave that jewel to Edward as a reward for helping him defeat one of his rivals."

"And what about this next one?" I sighed. "Is it

just as unimpressive as the others?"

In this manner, we moved from display to display, with me throwing out baseless insults, and Lestrade acting like the offended local. Before we knew it, we were standing outside and grinning at each other like a bunch of schoolkids who had managed to get away with pulling a prank on their teacher. The sky was still overcast, and thanks to a layer of low-hanging clouds visible directly above us, I had a feeling it was going to be raining in less than fifteen minutes.

"Curiosity is killing me," Lestrade admitted. "What'd you find in there?"

"I really don't know," I confessed. "I haven't looked at it yet. I barely had enough time to yank the tape off and shove it in my pocket when those people came up behind us."

Reaching into my jacket, I pulled out the crumpled piece of duct tape and noticed that whatever was meant to be hidden, it was small. As in, much smaller than the tape, so all I really saw was a lump. Shrugging, I handed the sticky mess to Jillian, who proceeded to carefully unfold the tape to reveal what her brother had hidden away.

I heard Jillian gasp with surprise. I still couldn't quite make out what she was holding, but I *did* see a flash of black. My first guess was that it was a black rubber washer, but once Jillian held it up to the light, allowing everyone to see it, I knew I was nowhere close. What was it? A ring. A black tungsten carbide ring!

"What is it?" Lestrade asked.

Jillian started sobbing. "It belonged to Joshua. This is my brother's ring! I don't think I've ever seen him take it off."

"Is it a wedding band?" I asked, curious. "I don't think I've ever seen one that color before."

Jillian shook her head. "No, he told me he bought this particular ring to show his commitment to the US Marines. The only mark on this ring is the laser-engraved Marines logo you can see here."

"And you're certain it belonged to your brother?" Lestrade asked.

"Without a doubt. Why in the world would Joshua leave his ring behind, and why would he leave it here, of all places?"

I held out a hand and watched as Jillian handed me her brother's ring. Placing the black piece of jewelry in my open palm, I squatted next to the dogs and held it out to them, curious as to what they would do. Sherlock approached first. He gave the item a few sniffs before turning to look at Watson, who also gave the ring a few sniffs. After a few moments, both dogs lost interest.

"Well, he left this behind and he even managed to get us to find it. What does that tell us?"

"That we're missing something," Lestrade murmured, more to himself than anyone else. "What was he trying to tell us?"

"What else can you tell us about this ring?" I asked, as I turned to Jillian. "You say Josh typically doesn't take this thing off. Well, what *did* he do with it? It has to mean something."

Jillian held up her hands in a helpless manner. "What that could be, I don't know, I'm afraid. Come on, Joshua. Why leave your ring behind?"

"Does it look like a wedding band to anyone else?" I asked.

"I told him that before, too," Jillian admitted. "Joshua always said it was because he was married to his work. The only thing I can tell you is that he chose this design for some purpose, only I don't know what that would be."

"It's heavier than most rings I've held," I decided. "Then again, I've never held one made of pure tungsten."

"How do you know for certain it's made of tungsten?"

I showed the ring to Lestrade. "Because, it says so on the inside of the ring, right here."

"What's wrong with the *G*?" Lestrade asked.

"Hmm? What's that?"

"Let me see the ring. Yeah, that's what I thought. See the rectangle, with the word *TUNG-STEN* inside? Tell me if you see anything that ... I don't know, stands out. I thought from my vantage point that it was smudged."

Holding the ring close to my face, I shook my head. "No, I don't see any ... whoa, Sherlock. I almost dropped it. Knock it off, would you? What's gotten into you?"

Sherlock nudged me again and whined. When I looked at him, though, the tri-colored corgi only had eyes for my hand, or, more importantly, what I was holding. Interested, I passed the ring from one hand to the other. Sherlock watched it as though it was the world's tastiest doggie biscuit.

"I do believe your canine companions are trying to tell you something," Lestrade said, grinning.

Sighing, I pulled out my phone and took a picture of the ring, just to humor the dogs. However, this was the part when the dogs would typically lose interest and move on to something else. Nope, not this time. Both Sherlock and Watson only had eyes for the ring, and wouldn't stop staring at it. Suggesting what, that there was something else we still needed to learn?

Again, I held up the ring and gave the inner side of Joshua's special black ring a close inspection. There, in a narrow rectangle, was the word Lestrade had noticed. Zeroing in on the *G*, I could see Lestrade had been right. That particular letter was different than the rest. It was almost as if … was it? Was it really different after all?

"What is it?" Jillian asked.

I showed her the ring. "Lestrade called it. The G of tungsten, here, is different. I'm trying to find out why."

"It's a mark, letting us know what it's made of?" Jillian asked, frowning. "Could there be another reason why it's here?"

I took back the ring. "If there's another reason, then I don't have any idea what it could ... well, hello! What do we have here?"

Jillian and Lestrade crowded close.

"What is it?" my fiancée asked.

"I'll be damned. All right, check this out. Look what happens if I put this ring on my thumb."

"Why your thumb?" Lestrade asked.

"Just humor me," I insisted. "Look. If I make sure it's nice and snug, and give it a small twist like this ... I was right! Look! Check out that word now!"

Jillian took the ring and gave a tiny gasp. The word tungsten now read TUNTSTEN. The letter had changed!

"How in the world did you know it could do that?" Lestrade demanded.

I nudged Jillian. "Hold the ring by pinching the inside and the outside. Yes, just like that. Now, while applying pressure to the inside, gently rotate the outer part of the ring."

"It moves!" Jillian exclaimed. She checked the ring. "Now there's a letter E showing!"

"Don't you get it?" I said, as I pointed at the ring. "Joshua sent us some type of message. We need to figure out what it says!"

FIVE

A re we reading too much into this?" Jillian asked, nearly an hour later. We had returned to the hotel and were currently crowded around the small desk facing the perimeter wall. Lestrade had gone home for the day. "What if it's just some random letters?"

"You spent the entire ride back here looking up those letters," I recalled. "Not only that, you went through it a second time, and even a third. Did the results change?"

"No."

"And you saw the same word I did, right? Do you really think it was put there by someone other than your brother?"

"No, not really."

"Good. Let's see the word you jotted down again, okay?"

Jillian passed me a slip of paper. Written on it

were the letters she found, in the order in which she found them:

E_GHT_@MG1N

That might look like a load of gibberish to you, and I wouldn't blame you for thinking that. However, if you reverse it, and then move that first E to the end, you get this:

EN1GM@_THG_

Now, *enigma*, I get. Joshua excelled at cryptography, which was just another way of saying he solved puzzles for a living. And puzzles? That was just another word for enigma. So, I knew without a shadow of a doubt that this message, er, *code* was in that ring because Joshua put it there. It was up to us to figure out what it meant.

"What's the THG for?" I wondered aloud. I glanced over at the dogs, but both were passed out on the bed. "Maybe it's short for something?"

Jillian shrugged. "Perhaps. I just have no idea what. Listen, it may be eight a.m. back home, but right now, it's four p.m. here. Are you interested in getting a bite to eat?"

"You have my attention. What about them?"

We both looked over at the dogs. Sherlock was paws up, and Watson was stretched out in the Flying Squirrel position next to him. Holding a finger to her lips, Jillian tilted her head in the dogs' direction.

"I don't think they're going anywhere, Zachary.

Besides, they're both snoring."

I pointed at the door. "Beautiful. Let's go. I just don't want to go too far. I don't want them waking up and making a fuss."

"How about we try the Blue Boar Pub?"

"I'm game. How far away is it?"

Jillian pointed straight down. "It's on the ground floor."

"Here in the hotel? That's perfect. After you, m'lady."

Jillian slipped her arm through mine. "Why thank you, kind sir."

Once we'd placed our orders and found a table, I took Jillian's hand in my own and gave it a reassuring squeeze.

"We're going to find your brother."

Jillian rested her head on my shoulder. "Thank you, Zachary. Somehow, I know we will. It doesn't stop me from worrying, though."

"Oh, I know it. We just need to …"

I trailed off as Jillian's phone began to ring. Hastily pulling it out, and ready to send it to voice mail, she caught sight of the display. "Oh! I do believe this is Staff Sergeant Murphy, the one I left a message for right after we landed. It looks like they're just now getting back to me."

"They're probably, just now, opening up their office."

Jillian's face turned ash-white as realization dawned. She had to have placed that call to the US Marines' office in the dead of night. No wonder she hadn't received an answer.

"Staff Sergeant Murphy! Thank you so much for calling me back. I am so sorry for calling so late. I … no, I'm sorry, I'm currently in London. Yes, sir, I'm investigating my … what's that? No, I most certainly will not. He is my brother, and since you were unwilling to help me look, I took it upon myself to look around. No, I'm not by myself. Of course not. My fiancé is with me. Yes, sir, that's him. We … hmm? Yes, we have found something, and we don't know what to do with it. No, it appears to be a code, or perhaps …"

"What is it?" I whispered, as I watched Jillian's eyes widen with shock.

Jillian jabbed a finger on her phone's mute button and looked up at me. "I think I know what that code is! It's a password!"

"For what?" I wanted to know.

Jillian unmuted her phone. "I'm sorry, Staff Sergeant. Zachary and I were having a quick word together. May I ask you something? Do marines have their own online accounts where they can store their own digital files?"

I nodded. Excellent question. Perhaps that code would allow access to …

"Oh, there isn't?" Jillian continued. "Shoot. I was hoping we'd be able to … I'm sorry? They all do? Thank you, you have been very helpful. Yes, I'll look into it. What's that? Well, yes, I suppose if I find anything, then I'll let you know. Thank you, Staff Sergeant."

"What is it?" I asked, hopeful we had a new lead.

"The military doesn't offer any of its members access to a digital repository," Jillian explained.

"Oh. Nuts."

"But," Jillian added, with a coy smile, "they do encourage their members to make use of online storage facilities."

"Such as ...?"

"Like Dropbox?" Jillian suggested. "Zachary, that code we found? I think it might be Joshua's password to his own personal account. Now that I think about it, he has mentioned having a Dropbox account on more than one occasion."

"We'd still need a username," I reminded her. "It's usually an email address. Do you happen to know what your brother uses?"

"I do. Oh, this is exciting! We have our first solid lead!"

Apparently, the Fates decided otherwise, and delivered a brutal reality check. Sitting in front of one the of hotel's public use computers, Jillian was having no luck in trying to sign-in to a Dropbox account that may, or may not, exist. Yes, Jillian claimed she'd heard her brother reference a Dropbox account, but there was no certainty that he was talking about his own. Perhaps there was one signed under another name?

And that, unfortunately, was the problem. There were too many unknowns. We could literally spend hours trying various usernames and email addresses, all with the code we found, and we would have no indication we were even on the right path.

"What are you using for a username?" I asked, nearly an hour later.

"It's the email address I know he has," Jillian answered, frowning. A look of determination had appeared on my fiancée's face and I could see that she was nowhere close to giving up. "I just don't know what to put."

"Have you been given any warnings that you're about to be locked out?"

Jillian nodded. "A few times. Why do you ask?"

I pointed at the seat. "May I try?"

"Of course."

Once seated, I pulled up the online storage company's home page and tapped the sign-in link. The log-on page appeared, I saw that Jillian had been jotting down notes as she tried various combinations. Good girl!

"Which of these have you tried the most?" I wanted to know.

Jillian tapped the third email address on the list. "This one. I received a message from him earlier this year from this particular account."

"Has he sent you any other messages from a different account?"

"No."

"And this same one is the one you've been focusing on?"

"Yes."

"What variations of the password have you

tried?"

"Variations?"

"Yeah. We don't know for certain what the beginning and ending letters are for this code, provided it *is* a password."

"Well, enigma is easy enough to figure out," Jillian said. "I'm not sure about the other part, so I put it at the end."

"All right, let's reverse it and put enigma at the end," I decided.

"I've tried that," Jillian said. "It didn't work."

"Did you put the underscore symbol after it?"

"I … oh. Er, I did not."

"I'm trying it now. Give me a moment. Wow, I think this computer is using a dial-up connection. Oh, hey, the screen changed! Jillian, we're in!"

"Omigod! Are you serious? May I sit there? I'd like to see what is in there."

This was her brother's account, and to tell the truth, I wasn't too comfortable poking around his files. I was only too happy to give up my seat.

While Jillian searched through the files Joshua had uploaded into his account, I took the dogs outside and let them do their business. Seeing a street vendor nearby, I wandered over and purchased a few bottles of soda. The UK, it would seem, was not a fan of Coke Zero, seeing how I couldn't find a bottle to save my soul. But, Diet Coke? That was available practically everywhere. Strangely enough, Pepsi was also difficult to come by, yet this tiny stand had several bottles, so I bought two. Slipping them into the water bottle holders on either side of my back pack, I tugged on the leashes.

"Let's go, guys."

"Cute dogs," the female proprietor said, after noticing both Sherlock and Watson were staring at her. "Can I give them a treat?"

"Umm, I'd have to ask you what you have in mind," I countered.

"I have a couple of small pieces of dried bread. My own dogs love them."

London's own version of doggie bagel bits. How cool!

"Oh, sure. Sherlock? Watson? The nice lady is offering you a treat. Would you care to …?"

Both dogs sat before I could finish the sentence.

"What well-trained dogs," the woman praised. "Here you go."

This is where I point out that neither dog bothered lifting their head, or even looked directly at the person offering them treats. Oh, they took them, don't get me wrong, but they seemed to be more interested in the actual tricycle-type device, with the built-in cooler, the woman was astride. Noticing the dogs' peculiar behavior, well, more peculiar than normal, I suppose, I gave the leashes another tug.

"Guys? Are you ready to go?"

"Thank you for the business," the woman said, as she prepared to depart. "Take good care of those dogs. Then again, I'm sure you get told that a lot."

"I do, yes. They're attention-loving pups, let me

tell you."

"Are they?" the woman inquired, tilting her head. "Are they puppies?"

"Oh, sorry. No, they're adults."

"They're so cute," the vendor gushed.

"I know it," I said, as I smiled at the lady. "You know it. The problem is, they know it, too. Thanks, again. I was beginning to give up hope that I could find a bottle of Pepsi. It's hard to come by in London."

Noticing the dogs still hadn't budged, I gave the vendor a questioning look, only she was already pulling away. Quickly snapping her picture, and one of the thing she was riding, I turned to the dogs and waggled the phone.

"There. Happy?"

That did the trick. The dogs were now the ones pulling their leashes, as though I had been the one holding things up. Whatever.

Jillian was eagerly waiting for me when I made it back to the hotel's lobby. She hurriedly motioned me over and indicated a chair. Then, she gasped with surprise as I pulled out the bottle of Pepsi.

"You found some!" Jillian exclaimed. "That's wonderful!"

"Found it at a vendor just outside," I said. "So, what did you find out?"

"Joshua wasn't the greatest at keeping records, and his files are rather disorganized, but I did find a rudimentary log of his that described the various projects he had been working on. Do you remember what I said about my brother loving puzzles?"

"Sure."

"Well, based on everything I've found, I can safely say he had a knack for locating items."

"Oh? What kind of items? Of the *missing* variety?"

"Exactly."

"Does it say anything about the silver chest?"

"It does, and how he suspected he was being followed. He doesn't mention who he got it from, or where he found it, but only that he suspected if he didn't get rid of it, then it was going to be taken back from him, by force, if necessary. That's why he drove to Wales."

"And that's why he shipped it to me," I deduced.

Jillian nodded. "I'd say so."

"Does he mention why he chose me?"

"No. I'm sure it's because he trusts you, Zachary."

"Well, I appreciate that," I began, "but we haven't even met. How could he trust someone he hasn't met?"

Jillian held up her left hand and wiggled her fingers. "Because, you're with me."

I shrugged. "That works for me. What *does* it say about that chest?"

Jillian returned her attention to the monitor. She clicked several files, opened several others, and then closed the majority of them. Of the one file that was still open, she tapped the screen as she began to read.

"Looks like he called it *Shamrock*."

I shrugged. "Makes sense."

"He tracked it from Dublin to London, and ended up at a place called CS."

"CS? Cryptex Solutions?"

"It doesn't say, but it does make sense."

"He found it there. Oh, this is starting to get good. What else do you have?"

"He suspected what the contents were, but was unable to open the chest. For the record, I'll bet he could have, since he's smarter than me."

"Maybe he didn't have a chance to work on it," I suggested.

"Possibly. Here's another reference for NO."

Thinking she had stopped in mid-sentence, I gave her an expectant look, only she returned my gaze with just as much curiosity as my own.

"What?"

"Isn't there more to that statement?"

"No."

"Yes."

"Huh?"

I looked up. "What was that?"

"I said, no, you said yes."

I nodded. "That's right. I wanted to know more about that statement, but you said no. I was hoping there was something else."

Jillian tapped her fingers on the desk as she studied me. "I think we're no longer on the same page. Let's try again. I found another reference for NO."

"Mm-hm, no *what*?"

"No what's, just NO."

"Okay, I'm lost. I feel like we're talking about *Who's on First?*"

Jillian shook her head. "I'm sorry, I'm talking about NO."

It was my turn to stare at my significant other. When it became clear I was hopelessly lost, Jillian smiled.

"NO," Jillian reiterated. "N-O."

"Ah. Joshua is calling something *NO*. Got it. Well, what's the reference?"

"I see a person's name: Davis Forrester, with the letters N-O next to it. With a question mark, of course."

I pulled out my phone and looked up the name. Searching for Davis Forrester didn't really give me any viable leads. However, as soon as I added London, my phone promptly returned a hit from a local news channel. There, on my screen, was a picture of a thirty-something guy with closely-cropped dark hair, a dark complexion, suggesting he had spent an inordinate amount of time outdoors, and wearing a black tuxedo jacket.

"What did you find?" Jillian asked, as she leaned over my shoulder.

I passed her the phone. "Just this guy. According to the article, Davis Forrester was gunned down in a mugging-gone-wrong."

"He's dead?"

"Looks that way."

"Well, that's tragic. How long ago did this happen?"

Jillian handed me back my phone. "Let's see. This was two months ago. Relevant?"

"I think so. Do you see this? And these three files over here, in this folder? Joshua had scanned in several pages of his notes. I have found DFs everywhere. Zachary, I think he might have known him."

I shrugged. "It's possible."

Sherlock chose that time to rise to his feet, stretch his back, and then return to his *down* position. Moments later, he rolled onto his back, as though we were all relaxing on the sofa back home. A few passing hotel patrons smiled down at the snoozing corgi as they headed to the front counter.

"Don't mind us," I quipped, offering the passersby a smile. "He's jet-lagged."

Jillian's hand suddenly gripped mine and she gasped. "Oh, you need to see this."

I returned my attention to the computer. "What is it?"

"I opened this folder, over here. It contains pictures. This first one? It's been named Istanbul2010."

"Istanbul. Turkey. All right, what about it?"

"Zachary, look at the picture."

Two soldiers, dressed in military fatigues, were smiling at the camera. Each had an arm around his companion. Both men were wearing camouflage flak jackets, and—conservatively—fifty pounds of gear strapped to their persons. Jillian tapped the dark-haired figure on the left.

"That's Joshua. And this one? Doesn't this look like Davis Forrester to you?"

"It sure looks like it," I said, as I leaned forward to give the picture a closer inspection.

Jillian held out her hand and waited for me to return my phone to her. "Yes, I'm positive these two pictures show the same man. This confirms it. My brother and this Davis Forrester were acquaintances."

Studying the picture on my phone's display, I could only nod. "So, they knew each other. Clearly friends. Hmm, do you think maybe Davis was helping your brother work on these projects?"

"Which suggests the possibility that, perhaps, Davis' being gunned down *wasn't* a case of being in the wrong place accidentally."

"It might explain why your brother has become so fixated on these types of cases," I suggested.

"It also means that, whoever NO is, they clearly don't like Joshua poking around and took steps to … to …"

I pulled Jillian in for a hug. "No, don't say it. We're not going down that road unless we absolutely have to. Until we hear otherwise, we're going to assume Joshua is being held somewhere, against his will."

"Oh, Zachary," Jillian sobbed, "what are we going to do?"

"Personally, I think the best way to find out what happened to your brother is to retrace his steps. If he's hiding somewhere, or if he's been taken by someone, then the best way to help him would be to solve whatever case he was working on."

Jillian nodded. "It makes sense."

"So, what is his most recent project?"

Jillian tapped the monitor's screen. "I'm not sure. He called his most recent project *Twins*. And, before you can ask, I can confirm I haven't found anything pertaining to some type of abduction or kidnapping case. It has to be a reference to some items."

"Or a pair of items," I added.

"Correct.

"Twins," I repeated. "That's not much to go on. That's all we have to work with?"

"It's all that was in the file. I don't know how far along he was."

"Maybe we should do a search for a pair of identical gems that might've been stolen," I suggested.

"Already did that. Nothing of the like."

"All right, what about the name of a stolen painting? Or sculpture?"

"Tried those, too. Still no luck."

"Wow, you're good, lady. Hmm, maybe *twins* refers to the name of a couple of cars?"

"I've tried searching for cars, boats, planes, and even remote control cars, boats, and planes. What else do you have?"

"We clearly think alike," I chuckled, thinking hard. What else could it be? My eyes alighted on the corgis and suddenly, I was nodding. "Animals? Pets?"

Jillian shook her head and sighed. "I thought of that, too. No such luck. I couldn't find any hits on anything of significance."

"Any insignificant items?" I asked.

"Nothing worth mentioning," Jillian said.

A thought occurred.

"Hey, does it say how many cases your brother has worked on? You said he has a knack for finding things. Besides the silver chest, what else has he found?"

Jillian sighed and sat back in her chair. "I've already looked. There are notes here for several cases. He doesn't go into too much detail. If I didn't know any better, then I'd assume it's done on purpose, in case someone manages to access this file. I'm guessing that is why he uses other words and phrases to describe his work."

"Like what?" I wanted to know.

Jillian returned to the computer and opened a file. "Take this one, for example. Joshua has named it *iceberg*. Why? What could it mean?"

"Do we know if these items have anything to do with ... I don't know, a treasure?" I asked. "Something valuable?"

"If it is, I have no idea what it could be about. Iceberg. Hmm. I'm not aware of any famous icebergs. What about you?"

"Only the one which sank the Titanic," I answered. "And, since the wreck of the Titanic was found years ago, I can't image it has anything to do with that ship."

"Iceberg," Jillian repeated, shaking her head. "I don't know. All right, here's another: Coronado. Any idea what that one could be referring to?"

"Iceberg and Coronado," I repeated, frowning. "Without some context, they could mean just about anything. We know he found the silver chest. I'd like to think that these other items are just as historically significant."

My fiancée fixed me with a stare. "Joshua has always said that the world's historical treasures belong in museums, and not in someone's private collection."

"I would agree."

Jillian tapped the screen. "Well, I think we should focus on this *Twins* case. If we can recreate Joshua's steps, then perhaps …?"

"… perhaps we can figure out which proverbial hole he fell into and pull him out?" I finished for her, after she trailed off.

"Exactly. Now, I did a search of his files for the word 'twins'."

"Did you find much?" I asked.

"Sadly, no, but I did find this. Let me show you. Now, in this file, which is just a basic text file, I found several references to someone named LSS. Know anyone with those initials?"

"I don't, no."

"All right, moving on. Here's something that's also interesting: *100 yrs* and *tx*. Joshua put it in bold."

"Looks like it reads one hundred years," I decided. "But, a hundred years for what? And *tx*? Texas?"

Jillian opened a browser on the computer and pulled up a popular search engine.

"Let's see what we can find out. I'll search for *twins*, *missing*, and I'll also throw in *Texas*. Now, let's see what we get."

The screen populated with the results. Turns out, there are lots of missing children in Texas. Jillian scrolled through the results and tried her luck on pages two and three. Nothing but faces of missing kids met our eyes.

"Well, that's depressing," I said.

Jillian was silent as she considered her options. A few moments later, she was tapping the backspace button as she cleared out her search and tried a new one.

"This time, let's search for *twins*, *Texas*, and *mystery*. Maybe we'll find some better hits?"

I twisted my index and middle fingers together on my right hand and waved it at her.

"Here's hoping."

It was also at this time that both dogs roused themselves from their nap and rose to their feet. Sherlock put his paws up on Jillian's lap so that he could see what was on the screen.

"Good morning, Sunshine," I said, as I ruffled

his fur.

I was ignored. Noticing Jillian had fallen silent, and was now ignoring me, too, I slid my chair close and gazed at the screen. There, on the display, was our answer: a Wikipedia entry for two cannons, both considered historical treasures to the state of Texas. Used in the Texas Revolution, during the battle of San Jacinto, the cannons were last seen in 1865, and are considered the Lone Star State's Holy Grail.

Jillian reached out and tapped the screen with a long, slender finger.

"What is it?" I asked.

"Lone Star State," Jillian repeated, indicating the passage I had just read.

"What about it?"

"LSS. Sound familiar?"

"Do you think those initials you found refer to Lone Star State?"

Jillian nodded. "I'm starting to. It looks like Joshua was tracking down the location of these two cannons. Can you imagine what the state of Texas would do to have these treasures back?"

I scrolled a little farther down the page. "We don't know for certain if they are even missing. See this? It says that one theory is that the cannons were melted down by the Union Army."

"It's just a theory," Jillian pointed out. Then she looked at Sherlock, who was still propped up on his hind legs. "And then we have *them*. They've taken notice of what we're doing. Would that not indicate we're on the right track?"

I gave each of the dogs a pat. Sighing, I pulled my phone out and took a picture of the flippin' computer screen, which mollified the dogs. Settling back on the floor, I was about to slide my phone into my pocket when I noticed a text file in the same folder as the pictures. What would a text file be doing in there? And with *that* particular name?

I placed a hand over Jillian's, which was holding the mouse. "Hold off closing that one, would you? Do you see that?"

"The text file?"

"Yes. See the name?"

"CHST!" Jillian exclaimed. "How did I not notice that before?"

I watched my fiancée click the file, but as soon as the word processing program opened, we received an error. Apparently, the file couldn't be opened. Jillian sighed and sat back.

"Oh, well, we tried."

"Wait a moment," I told her as I stared at the file on the screen. "There are any number of reasons why you can't open that file. Yes, the file could be bad, but the file might also have the incorrect extension."

"Are you suggesting Joshua deliberately changed the file type?" Jillian asked.

"Look at the name of the file," I insisted. "What do you think?"

"What should I change it to?" Jillian asked, as

she opened the computer's settings and enabled file extensions to be visible.

I shrugged. "How about a picture?"

The *txt* extension was replaced with *jpg*.

No luck.

"I know pictures come in various formats," I said, trying to sound like I knew what I was talking about. "Try a different one."

Jillian tried every format she could think of, which included several I didn't know were even picture files, but nothing worked. After a few moments had passed, a notion dawned: maybe it wasn't a picture file?

"How big is it?"

Jillian checked the file size. "Nearly thirty megabytes."

"That's one mother of a text file," I decided. "Perhaps it might be a video file?"

We struck gold on the third extension we tried. Just like that, we were suddenly looking at a new window, with Joshua's face smiling back at us. Jillian sucked in a breath and shakily reached for the mouse to click on the *Play* button.

"Bet I've got you thinking now, huh, Jilly-Bear?" Josh's voice said.

"Jilly-Bear?" I softly repeated.

"Hush," Jillian whispered.

"If you're watching this, then I can only assume Zack received the chest and was able to open it. Good for him. Good for you two, actually. I knew I sent it to the right person."

"I just wanna know how he got his hands on it," I murmured.

"Hush."

"By now, you've had time to poke through my files. All I'm going to say is what I've told you from day one: the world's treasures do *not* belong in the hands of private collectors. Time is running out. Jillian? Iceberg and Coronado are within reach. With luck and perseverance, I will have found them by the time you view this video. As for the Twins?"

"Come on," Jillian urged. "Tell us about the Twins!"

"The Twins are safe, but I am not. Chest isn't happy, but it serves 'em right. I've just about collected enough evidence to bring them down once and for all. But, if you're watching this, then it can only mean I'm on the run. Do *not* try to find me. I can take care of myself."

The video abruptly ended. Jillian, understandably, was sobbing. He didn't want us looking for him? And he can take care of himself? I had a feeling that my future brother-in-law had bitten off more than he could chew.

Collars jingled as Sherlock and Watson gave themselves a good shaking, which typically meant they were ready to go. Handing the leashes to Jillian, I logged out of Joshua's storage account and, together, we quickly headed for the elevators.

"Are you thinking what I'm thinking?" I asked, dropping my voice to a whisper.

"Someone got to him first," Jillian sniffed.

"My thoughts exactly. Don't worry. We'll find him."

SIX

"Why are we back here again?" I asked. It was the following day and here we were, before a very familiar landmark. "We were already here. We found your brother's ring here. I doubt he left any other clues."

Jillian nodded. "I know that. However, this is the last place we know he went to. This would be the place to start."

"At the Tower of London? And how are we supposed to pick up the scent—so to speak—from a case that has probably gone cold by now?"

"Think about it," Jillian urged. "If Joshua had more time, or let's say he believes he's now no longer being followed, don't you think he would have gone back for his ring?"

"Yeah, well ... all right, you have me there," I admitted. "So, we're here, and he isn't. Where do we start?"

Right on cue, both Sherlock and Watson perked

up. Their ears swiveled left and right, as though they were trying to figure out which direction a new noise was coming from. Just like that, I watched Sherlock's ears turn forty-five degrees to the right and stay there. A few moments later, Watson's were the same.

"All right, I'll bite. What do you guys hear? I don't hear anything that could ..."

I trailed off as the dogs leapt to their feet and physically pulled me, whether I wanted to tag along or not. Glancing over my shoulder, I saw that Jillian and Lestrade, who had joined us just minutes ago, fell into step behind me. From the angle I was being pulled, I could see we were headed for the closest street, where several of London's trademark black taxis were waiting for fares.

"Do we know if Joshua took a taxi from here?" I asked, as I looked back at Lestrade.

"I've already checked, mate," Lestrade returned. "And the answer is no. No cabbies reported anyone matching Joshua Cooper's description being picked up anywhere around this area."

"Maybe he had rented a car?" Jillian suggested.

"A good suggestion, but no, I checked that, too. He hasn't rented any cars."

"Maybe he's borrowed a car from a friend?" I suggested, as Sherlock and Watson strolled past all the waiting cabs. I would've sworn we were headed for a taxi. "What about a motorcycle?"

"Joshua hated motorcycles," Jillian said, shaking her head.

"What about his friend, that Davis fellow?" I asked. "Could he be using someone else's car?"

"Who is this Davis person you're talking about?" Lestrade wanted to know.

"Davis Forrester," Jillian answered. "We discovered he and my brother knew each other and were probably friends."

"When did you discover this?" Lestrade asked, frowning. "How come I wasn't notified?"

"Because we just figured that out last night," I said, as I continued to let the dogs lead. Now it looked as though we were headed for an area around fifty feet away, which had several small ticket booths set up, racks of pamphlets and flyers, and a small crowd of people milling about. "I knew we were all meeting up this morning, so we didn't want to trouble you with something that may, or may not, be important."

"What else have you learned about this Davis person?" Lestrade wanted to know.

"Well, from what we could tell, Joshua and Davis served in the military together," Jillian said, "and more than likely, Davis' death was probably not a chance incident."

Lestrade's phone appeared in his hand. "Mr. Forrester is dead? Let me check some details."

We arrived at the small group of people, which consisted of two family groups. Both of them had small kids with them, and all of them, adults included, turned to look at the dogs.

"Corgis!" one of the mother's exclaimed. She

had an accent, but it wasn't British. Australian? "Oh, I love these dogs. They're so cute!"

Watson stopped long enough to get a few pats and scratches. Sherlock ignored everyone, which I thought was odd, and headed straight for a small, rotating wire display full of tourist pamphlets. Stopping at the display of popular attractions, I glanced down at the dogs, only to see them staring at the middle section of the rack. What was on it? Excursions to Stonehenge, the Tower Bridge, and a few places I hadn't heard of, which were to the west and to the north. Sherlock then looked at the ticket booth.

"What, you want to go on a tour? Now?"

"What's going on?" Jillian asked, as she appeared next to me. She looked at the ticket booth and gave the dogs a skeptical look. "They want us to buy a ticket?"

"This doesn't make any sense," Lestrade added.

I shrugged and pulled out my wallet. "Hey, we have a fifty-fifty shot here. Either we get lucky, or we don't. Besides, if you're being followed, this is a great way to hide."

"How's that?" Lestrade asked.

I pointed at one of the three red double-decker buses parked nearby. "By disappearing into a tour group."

"Big Bus Tours operates hundreds of buses throughout London," Lestrade argued. "If Lieutenant Cooper bought a ticket, which I already know he hasn't, then how in the bloody hell would we know which bus he got on?"

I pointed at the dogs. "I trust them to know."

"That's a long shot," Lestrade informed me. "Even for your amazing dogs."

"Let's just see what happens. Guys? Look. I'm buying tickets, okay? Hey, there. I need three tickets for ... do you allow dogs on the bus?"

The young teenager manning the booth nodded. "Sure. Dogs are allowed, provided they can either sit on your lap or fit under the seat. For safety's sake, we can't have them blocking the aisles."

"Got it. They're corgis, so they won't be a problem, isn't that right?"

Both Sherlock and Watson panted at me as they watched me arrange our next leg of the journey.

"Three adult tickets, please."

Sliding my credit card through their machine, I handed slips of paper to Jillian and Lestrade.

"Here you go. Now, we just need to ... all right, looks like we're off. Sherlock? Watson? Pick us a good bus, okay?"

We headed out, with the corgis in the lead, only we didn't make it far. The dogs stopped at another rack of pamphlets and flyers, and before I could pull them away, Sherlock and Watson immediately sat. Sighing, I leaned close to inspect the offerings. This one had longer trips, namely three hours or more. Seeing how the dogs were preparing to drop into a *down* position, I reached for my phone and snapped a few pictures before either of them could make themselves too comfortable. My two dogs stared up at the various tourist destinations and excursions, looked back at me, snorted once, and presto, we were on the move again.

The tickets we purchased were for some type of program called *Hop On, Hop Off*, which essentially meant that our tickets were good for their entire bus line in the city. We would be able to get off the bus, er, *hop off* the bus at any point, and then, if so desired, we could *hop on* again if we wanted to go to another destination. However, these special tickets were only for today's date, so if we were going to be checking out multiple parts of the city, then we had best get going.

"Pick one, guys," I told the dogs. "Left, middle, or right, I don't care. Just ... and we're heading right. Jillian? Still with me?"

"I'm right behind you," came my fiancée's voice.

"Lestrade?"

"Still here, and if this pans out, then I will personally give the four of you a personalized tour through London."

Grinning, I looked at Jillian and we knocked knuckles.

"You're on, pal. Sherlock? Watson? Is this the one you want to go on?"

In response, the dogs headed for the steps leading up, into one of three buses parked in a row. What this one had over the other two, I didn't know. Selecting seats near the midway point, we settled back, into our chairs, and waited for the tour to start. Catching sight of the equivalent of a conductor, and remembering that the dogs were not allowed in the aisles, I motioned for Watson to jump up, onto my lap, and then Sherlock. Once the dogs were situated, we presented our tickets, saw them punched, and then we watched as the uniformed guard reached into a storage compartment behind the driver's seat and pull out a headset, followed by a large bag. Squinting, I could make out earbuds, individually wrapped.

"You'll want to plug them into those ports there," I was told. "The tour will start shortly. Cute dogs!"

Sherlock and Watson wriggled with delight.

Sitting back in my seat, clutching my fiancée's hand tightly in my own, I wondered how long we'd be on this bus. The question was, how long was Joshua here? Assuming the dogs were correct —and let's face it, they usually are—Joshua was on one of these buses for an unknown amount of time, presumably to hide from someone actively pursuing him. So, either he hung out on the bus while he figured out what to do, or else saw something which forced him to bail off.

Jillian squeezed my hand. "Penny for your thoughts?"

"Oh, I was just wondering how long your brother was on this bus. Was he looking for a place to relax, was he hiding from someone, or ...?"

"... or was he just moving from point A to point B?" Lestrade finished, as he turned in his seat to look over at us. "I've been wondering that, too. I'm also wondering how we didn't pick up the possibility that Mr. Cooper could have used one of these buses instead of a cab."

"I wouldn't worry about it," I told our British friend. "Unless something pans out here, then we ..."

I trailed off as I caught sight of the dogs. Sherlock had just fired off a warning woof. Suddenly, both dogs were vying for the best spot to see out the windows, which meant both were jockeying for unobstructed views. Seeing both corgis dancing around on Jillian's lap, I managed to pull Sherlock over to me and hold him in place. Needless to say, he wasn't impressed.

"Awwoooooowooooowoowoo!" Sherlock complained.

Jillian giggled. "Wow. How many was that?"

"I counted four," I answered, referring to the number of syllables in Sherlock's howl. The higher the number, the more frustrated Sherlock happened to be. "What do you think?"

Jillian reached for the red-handled lever labeled *Stop*.

"Time to go!"

"Are you sure?" Lestrade asked, as he looked back, through the rear windows, at the ticket kiosk still visible down the street. "That was what, maybe five minutes at the most?"

"Perhaps Joshua felt he was being followed?" Jillian said, as the two of us rose to our feet and headed for the door. "Or, maybe he *knew* he was."

Standing on the side of Palace Street, we watched the big red bus disappear into the distance. Sighing, I looked down at the dogs, who were standing motionless, alert. If I didn't know any better, I'd say they expected to see a boogeyman jump out at them at any time.

"That was a waste of money," I lamented.

"You never know, Zachary," Jillian said. "Those tickets are good for the whole day. They allow us to get back on any of that company's buses."

"Well, there is that. Guys? You wanted us off the bus. Here we are, next to ... holy cow! Is that Buckingham Palace?"

Lestrade turned to look behind us. He nodded, and then pointed at the closest street sign.

"Appropriately named, don't you think? Palace Street? Yes, this is the palace. You should see it up close. Not many are fortunate enough to be able to say they have seen the inside."

"Have you?" I asked, as I watched the dogs turn left and head southeast on Palace Street.

"Have I what, been inside the palace?" Lestrade smiled and nodded once. "I have, yes. It's an experience you'll treasure for the rest of your lives. Where are we going? Does anyone know?"

I looked down at the dogs and shrugged. Pointing at the street in front of us, I turned to Lestrade and grinned. "We seem to be headin' thataway."

"And you expect us to just follow your dogs as they lead you to ... where are we going? Do you know?"

"I don't, sorry," I told Lestrade. "Tell you what, as soon as they learn to answer me, you'll be the first to know." Hearing nothing coming from our liaison, I glanced over to see Lestrade shaking his head. Sherlock let out a snort and then pulled harder. "Hang on, boy. We'll get there. We don't need to run, all right?"

At least, I *hoped* we didn't have to run.

"Would you mind answering a question?" Jillian said, as she turned to Lestrade.

"If I can, ma'am. Go ahead."

"How long has Joshua been in London?"

"He's a frequent traveler."

"Yes, I know that. You didn't answer the question, so let me rephrase it. How long has Joshua been here on this, his most recent trip?"

"I see what you're asking," Lestrade said, nodding. "Nearly a month."

"How often does he come here?" I asked. I was pretty sure I knew where Jillian was going with this.

"He spends a lot of time here," Lestrade admitted. "Why do you ask?"

"Why doesn't he have a car?" Jillian asked.

"Why doesn't he have his own place?" I asked, at the same time.

Nope. Definitely not on the same page. Same book, yes, but different chapters.

I pointed at Jillian. "Ladies first. If Joshua is here all the time, why didn't he have his own car? It'd have to be inconvenient as heck to constantly rely on someone else to get you to where you need to go."

"We tried," Lestrade said, giving us a sheepish smile. "Cooper wouldn't hear of it. He said he was perfectly fine taking a bus or a cab."

Jillian was nodding. "Joshua can be stubborn, so that sounds like something he'd say. Very well, what about Zachary's question? Why didn't my brother have his own apartment? Why would he be staying at a hotel?"

"Again, we tried. We even assigned him a flat, all expenses paid. He badgered us to do it his way."

"And what is *his* way?" I asked.

"It's what I admired most about him," Lestrade confessed. "His incredible ability to not back down from something he believes in. He insisted he stay in public accommodations and wouldn't take no for an answer."

"Was he staying there on his own dime?" I asked. We were approaching an intersection and I was preparing to cross the street when I felt the leashes go taut. Looking down, I saw that the dogs wanted to cross, too, but in the other direction. Apparently, we were supposed to follow this new road northeast. "Wait, guys. We can't just go trotting off, across the road. We have to wait until we're allowed, all right?"

Sherlock snorted with exasperation.

"The only way my superiors agreed to your brother's demands, Miss Cooper," Lestrade finally said, answering Jillian's question, "was that he submit his expenses at the end of each month. Whether or not he did, I don't know, I'm afraid. I never inquired."

My fiancée sighed. "Oh, Joshua. What have you gotten yourself into?"

We waited an additional three minutes before the sign changed and it became safe to proceed.

"I've always dreamed of exploring a new city like this," Jillian said, which I knew was a concerted attempt to lighten her mood. "Foreign country, different driving habits, and quaint little restaurants. Take this one, for example. Do you smell that? I don't know what it is, but it smells heavenly."

"Pssht," I snickered. "I would recognize that smell anywhere."

Lestrade nodded. "Fish and chips. There's a shop just around the corner. I will attest to the quality of their food, since I've been there so many times I think I have my own table."

I looked down at the dogs. "Do they have outdoor seating?"

"They do. I'm all for getting a bite to eat. Ma'am?"

"Please call me Jillian, and yes, I could eat."

Twenty minutes later, we were seated on an exterior patio, with glasses of lemonade for Lestrade and Jillian, while I had a nice, refreshing, super-bad-for-me diet soda. Watching the people pass by, I turned to Jillian and took her hand.

"How are you holding up?"

"It's difficult," Jillian admitted. "I don't like knowing Joshua could be out there, somewhere, in serious trouble. What if he's hurt? Or ... or ..."

The waitress arrived right then, with our order. She noticed our drinks were half-full and promptly took them away to be refilled.

"No, don't say it," I ordered. "We will not be crossing that particular bridge unless we have to. Oh, wow, this is really good!"

"I'm surprised," Lestrade said. "I didn't think many Americans would enjoy British-style fish and chips."

"What's the difference between the two?" I asked. "What sets one apart from the other?"

"Type of fish and the batter used," Jillian answered, as if she was responding to a trivia question on a game show. "Usually cod or haddock, I believe."

"You believe correctly," Lestrade said, bowing. "My mum made really good fish and chips. Light, airy beer batter, thick wedges for the chips, and ..."

The waitress returned, with our drinks.

"... this place *miiiight* be better than hers. Don't ever tell her I said that."

Jillian and I took our first bite. Oh, I've had some good fish and chips back home in the States, but this? This is a battle we lose to the British. Light, crunchy batter and flavorful chips, enjoyed in the company of friends in another country. Man, it doesn't get any better than this. That was when I noticed the blob of green on my plate. Curious, I leaned forward for a better look.

"Mushy peas," Lestrade said, taking up a spoonful of his own. "Very traditional, and very good."

"Peas? Smooshed peas? Really?"

"Mushy peas," Lestrade corrected. "Mature peas left to dry in the fields rather than being picked."

"Marrowfat peas," Jillian explained. "They are soaked overnight …"

"… for at least eight hours," Lestrade interjected.

"Right. After eight hours, then they're cooked on low. Add in a little cream, and they are to die for. Greg, are you a cook?"

Lestrade shook his head. "My mum. She's a whiz in the kitchen. Zack? What's with the face? Not a fan of peas?"

"He's not a fan of green," Jillian said, laughing.

"Green? Oh, you mean green food? Nonsense. Some of the best food is green."

"Name one," I told our British friend.

Lestrade pointed at his plate. "That's easy. You're looking at one."

"Besides that one," I argued.

"Green beans. Brussel sprouts."

"Zucchini," Jillian added.

"Ah, yes. Wonderful. Oh, to have a home in the country with a garden to grow your own vegetables."

"I have such a place back home," Jillian said. "My garden produces many fresh vegetables, which I usually end up sharing with all my neighbors."

The waitress wandered by, saw that our drinks were low, and started collecting glasses. Watson looked up at the waitress and wiggled her rear in anticipation of a good scratching.

"He's so cute!"

I smiled up at the woman as she collected our glasses, but then watched Sherlock lift his head from his *down* position to stare at our server. Sherlock then turned to give me a neutral look.

"What?" I asked, as though I expected an answer from the corgi.

Sherlock let out a snort, turned to look at our waitress once more, and then settled back to the ground.

"What was that all about?" Jillian inquired.

"Haven't the foggiest. Hmm. Hand me my phone, would you? Hey, uh, Isabella, is it? Have you worked here long?"

"Better part of two years," the woman cheerfully told us. "Is there something I can do for you, love?"

"It sounds like there's a better than average chance you were here when a friend of ours was passing through," I said, as I pulled up a photo of Josh on my phone. Holding up my cell and allowing Isabella to see the display, I let out a cautious sigh. "By any chance, do you remember if this guy was here?"

The woman visibly brightened as she gazed at the picture. Within moments, she was smiling.

"Oh, yes, I remember him, I do. Such a sweetie."

All three of us perked up. The dogs, I might add, lost interest and returned to their naps. Lestrade stared at Sherlock and Watson for a few moments before shaking his head.

"All right. You've made a believer out of me. That was amazing!"

"When did you see him last?" Jillian asked.

A look of concern spread over the server's features. "Oh, bloody hell. You're his wife, aren't you? Blast it all to …"

"My name is Jillian," my fiancée explained, "and I'm his sister."

Relief washed over Isabella's face, only to be quickly replaced by apprehension. "Has something happened to him?"

"Possibly," I said, drawing Isabella's attention. "We're trying to retrace his steps. How long ago did you see him?"

"Less than two weeks ago," Isabella decided.

"Do you typically remember every customer who comes in here?" Lestrade asked.

"When you look like that, I do," Isabella murmured, blushing.

"Did he give any indication where he was headed?" Jillian asked.

"No, I'm sorry, love, he didn't."

"How was he behaving?" Lestrade asked.

Isabella frowned. "Behaving?"

"Happy, scared, relaxed, or …?" I offered.

"Oh, all right. He seemed fine. Ate his dinner

here. I flirted with him. I swear he flirted right back, so it gave me hope that someone like him, who could pass for a movie star, by the way, and someone like me could get together. What's happened to 'im? Tell me, please!"

"He didn't report for work," I explained, thinking fast. "It's nothing for you to worry about. He's probably had one too many. We were hoping he might've mentioned which bar he was planning on visiting."

Surprisingly, Isabella was almost immediately shaking her head. "No, no bar for him, poor fella. I could tell he was tired. Kept sayin' he was lookin' forward to getting back."

"Getting back?" Lestrade asked. He was holding, like all detectives would under these circumstances, a small notebook, and was scribbling like crazy. "Getting back to where, did he say?"

"What are you, a cop?"

Lestrade flashed his badge and nodded. "Detective Sergeant Gregory Lestrade, ma'am. Do go on."

"Yes. Yes, of course. That lovely bloke was lookin' forward to getting' back to his flat, I'm sure of it."

"Did he say, or do anything else that might've led you to believe he had other plans?" Jillian asked.

Isabella had started shaking her head no even before Jillian had finished asking her question.

"Not much chance of it, if you ask me."

"Thank you for your help," I told our waitress,

giving her my friendliest smile. "You've been incredibly helpful."

"I have? Well, fancy that. You're welcome. Let me know if you need anythin' else."

After Isabella had wandered off, both Jillian and I looked down at the dogs.

"It's so very impressive, guys," I said, lowering my voice. "I wish I knew how you do it."

"Where do they want to go now?" Lestrade asked, after we had finished our lunch and paid the check.

Glancing down at our canine companions, I shrugged. "Hmm. Isabella insisted Joshua wanted to get back. Get back *where*? If I were to venture a guess, and since our waitress mentioned Joshua looked tired, then I'd say he was planning on going back to the hotel. That's where I say we should go, but you know what? The dogs haven't let us down yet. Let's see where they want to go next. Sherlock? Watson? You're up, guys."

Once we left the pub, we continued along Castle Lane for another fifteen minutes until we encountered a much larger, much busier street. According to a nearby street sign, we had found a road by the name of B323. What the B stood for, I didn't know, nor did I ask. Byway?

The dogs pulled on their leashes. They wanted to go right. Verifying Jillian and Lestrade were still following us, we started out at a healthy clip when, much to my surprise, the dogs indicated they wanted to make an immediate left. Turning to look at Jillian, I shrugged.

"We're turning again."

"That was quick," Jillian observed.

"We're now at Petty France," Lestrade said, as he scribbled more notes in his notebook. "Can I ask how much farther we're going to go? I can always send for a car. It'd be quicker."

"And run the risk of missing something?" I asked, as I turned to look at our British friend. "You saw what they were able to do back there, at that fish and chips shop. Somehow, Sherlock and Watson are managing to retrace Joshua's steps. I'd rather not miss anything else, so you can order a car, if you'd like. We can meet up when we make it back to the hotel later today."

"And have to report to my superiors that I deserted the two of you? No, thank you. The car can wait."

We were on Petty France ... let me pause here a moment. I thought there were some strange street names back in the States, but Petty France? Who was responsible for naming the streets around here? Anyway, we continued along this particular road, looking like a strange, extended family taking the corgis for a walk, when the leashes went taut again. This time, we were at another intersection, and the dogs wanted to turn right.

"It's Broadway!" Jillian exclaimed, delighted. "My, aren't you two the smartest doggies in the whole wide world?"

"What'd I miss?" I asked. "What's on Broadway?"

Jillian pointed across the street. "Really? Doesn't any of this look familiar to you?"

"And you're testing me," I groaned. "Come on. We already know how bad my sense of direction is."

"We're back at the hotel!" Lestrade exclaimed. He dropped into a squat and scratched each dog behind their ears. Both corgis, I might add, were drooling by the time he was done. "You two are simply amazing!"

"We're at the hotel?" I asked, looking around. "Where do you see the … oh. Duh. It's right in front of my face. All right, in my defense, we came from an entirely different direction."

"No, we didn't," Jillian argued. "We left the hotel, headed down this very street, and then turned left, which would be …?"

"Petty France," I groaned. "Don't look at me like that, Lestrade. It's the story of my life. I'm always getting lost."

"But not with them," our British friend decided, as he looked at the dogs. "It makes me wonder."

"What?" Jillian prompted.

"Could the dogs have picked up your brother's scent? Is that how they were able to follow him so effectively?"

"Sherlock and Watson have never met Joshua," Jillian pointed out. "And there's nothing here with his scent, so we know that didn't happen."

"Besides," I added, "the trail is way too old.

You're talking about trying to follow a scent, in a city this size, that many days ago? Dogs have a great sense of smell. However, not even *they* are that good."

"Then, how did they do it?" Lestrade wanted to know.

"As soon as you learn to speak corgi," I returned, "you be sure to ask them, okay? And, should they answer, I would love to hear how they do it, too."

Stepping inside the hotel, we made it halfway to the elevators when the girl behind the counter, who happened to be Allyson, from before, caught up with us. Judging from the wheezes and the overwhelming sense of being flustered, I could only imagine she was waiting for us to walk in the door. Only, when we came in, I did remember her helping an elderly couple. I did find out, later, that Allyson had *sprinted* the thirty feet or so in order to get in front of us as soon as possible.

Both corgis perked up. Based on the abruptness of the clerk's arrival, I'm surprised the dogs didn't bark at her. And, oddly enough, Allyson had a frightened, crazed look in her eyes. She refused to look directly at me. Instead, she chose to stare at the floor.

"Is there something we can help you with?" I asked.

"I ... I ..."

"I'm guessing there's something you need us to do," I chuckled, as the three of us waited for the girl to catch her breath.

"I have … there is …"

For the first time, I noticed Allyson was holding something. What was it? It was an envelope, and even from where I was standing, I could see a red, embossed logo on the front of it, with a very recognizable name: WINDSOR CASTLE.

"This … came for you," Allyson stated, trying valiantly to catch her breath. "You never … told me you were celebrities, Mr. Anderson!"

Taking the proffered envelope, I ran my finger along the seam to break the seal.

"What do you have there?" Jillian asked. She caught sight of the logo and gasped. "Is that what I think it is?"

I handed her the letter inside. "None other. The Queen of England, it would seem, has grown tired of waiting for us to contact her. She's informing us that our audience will be taking place very soon."

"When?" Jillian wanted to know. "It's not today, is it? I am nowhere near ready."

I tapped the paper. "We have a reprieve, but not for long. Looks like we're going to be meeting the Queen tomorrow morning, at ten a.m."

SEVEN

Y ou do realize that we have a problem? Or, more specifically, that *I* have a problem? I can't meet with the Queen tomorrow!"

Alarmed, Jillian looked over at me. "What's the matter? We knew we would be meeting the Queen, so it shouldn't come as a surprise that ... oh. Oh!"

"What's going on?" Lestrade wanted to know. "What did I miss?"

Opening the door to our room, and holding it open so that both Jillian and Lestrade could enter, I pointed at our suitcases, currently sitting in the closet as I passed them by.

"Right there. There's the problem. Do you see a garment bag in there?"

"Er, no. I do see several pieces of luggage."

"This is the Queen of England," I reminded my British friend. "I can't walk into Buckingham Palace wearing what I'm wearing now. Come on, would that be appropriate?"

Lestrade sighed. "I've seen it before, I'm sorry to say. Kudos to you, my American friend, for recognizing the importance of the occasion."

"Made you cringe, didn't it?" I challenged.

"It did, yes. Very well. You appear to have a problem."

"Thanks, Captain Obvious."

"You know what this means, don't you?" Jillian asked.

I groaned aloud. "We have to go shopping."

"We get to go shopping," Jillian said, at the same time.

"You say it as though shopping is a bad thing," Lestrade laughed. Seeing my expression, he sobered. "Is it? Oh, I get it. You don't care for shopping, is that it?"

"He shops like he's on a scavenger hunt," Jillian laughed. "Men just don't appreciate the fine art of shopping."

"Now, I wouldn't go that far," Lestrade chuckled. "I don't mind an occasional outing, but I'm not one to waste time browsing for something I don't need."

I grinned at the detective. "Well said, amigo."

Jillian swatted my arm. "Oh, Zachary, please. You make it sound like shopping is akin to getting your teeth pulled."

Lestrade grinned. "My wife likes to shop, but I don't believe she's that passionate about it.

I hooked a thumb at Jillian. "She coined the

phrase *shop 'til you drop*. I'd rather get in, get what you need, and get out."

"We need a store specializing in slightly over-sized shirts," Jillian said, turning to Lestrade. "Zachary has a long torso, and broad shoulders, which means he wears either a 2XLT or a 3XL. Preferably, he looks better in the 2XLT, because the 3XLs tend to flare open around the waist."

"There's a John Banks not too far from here, I believe," Lestrade said. "Brooklyn is a little farther away, but they also have a nice selection of large clothing."

"Starting to feel like a whale here," I grumped. "Just one of the many reasons why I don't care for clothes shopping."

"John Banks?" Jillian repeated, as she gathered up her purse. "Thank you very much. We'll try there first."

"Now, wait a moment," I protested. "What about the dogs? I'm pretty sure we're not going to be allowed to take them into the stores around here, and let's face it, no one is going to believe they're service dogs."

Lestrade raised a hand. "I'd be more than happy to watch your canine companions for you while you ... *shop*."

"You're enjoying this, aren't you?" I mock-accused.

Lestrade grinned. "Whatever do you mean, good sir?"

Jillian suddenly sobered. She turned to Lestrade

and raised a hand. "Have you ever met the Queen?"

Me, Sherlock, and Watson all turned to regard the detective sergeant. Surprisingly, Lestrade was nodding.

"I have, yes."

"How many times?" I asked.

"Nearly a dozen. Why do you ask?"

"Do most people in your position have that frequent contact with the Queen?" Jillian asked.

Lestrade shrugged. "I suppose some do."

"But, you do," Jillian pressed.

"Where are you going with this?" I pressed, as I turned to Jillian. "What's the matter?"

"Well, I just wondered when he was going to admit that he's here, working undercover on the Queen's order."

I gave Lestrade a speculative look. "He already admitted that he's been assigned to look after us. Isn't that type of work considered being undercover? He told us we could call him Lestrade, but I get the impression that wasn't his real name. Why does it matter?"

"I was told she was sharp," our British friend said, by way of explanation. "Ms. Cooper? You are correct."

"Why didn't you tell us?" I asked.

"Because, you didn't ask."

I held up a hand. "Wait. That means the Queen knows we've been here ever since we landed, doesn't it?"

"What do you think?" Lestrade challenged.

"Does she know anything about my brother?" Jillian wanted to know.

"That is beyond my security level, I'm afraid."

I gave Lestrade a friendly nudge on his shoulder. "You weren't kidding, were you? You've met the Queen a number of times?"

"That's right. Why do you ask?"

"Can you give us some pointers?" I asked.

"Oh, you mean, what to say and do in her presence?"

I nodded. "Yes, please. Do we bow? Curtsy?"

"There are no obligatory forms of greeting in place when meeting Her Majesty the Queen."

"But ..."

"Just a moment," Lestrade said, interrupting me. "There are those who wish to observe traditional forms. For men, this is accomplished with a neck bow. Head only, mind you."

"What about the women?" Jillian asked.

"Women may make a small curtsy," Lestrade answered. "However, I wouldn't."

"You wouldn't *what*?" I asked, curious.

"I wouldn't bow," Lestrade said. "Or curtsy, if I was a woman. It's generally accepted nowadays that civilians do not bow or curtsy before Her Majesty. If I were you, I would just extend a simple handshake, but don't attempt it unless she offers it first. Understood?"

I nodded. "Understood. Listen, will there be anyone else present besides the Queen?" Jillian gave me a curious glance. "It's only to steer me in the right direction in case I goof something up. I really don't want to embarrass my country, or insult a royal. Go figure, huh?"

"To answer your question, there will always be someone nearby," Lestrade said. "Now, I don't think there's anyone there whose job it is to make certain visitors don't insult Her Majesty the Queen. Therefore, I'd start reviewing the Dos and Don'ts of meeting our Queen."

"The Dos and Don'ts?" I repeated. "Where do I find those?"

"Where else? The Internet, of course."

"Walked into that one," I grumbled.

"May I make one final suggestion?" Lestrade asked, giving Jillian a smile as he did so.

Jillian took my hand as we both nodded. "Please do."

"Zack? I'd find something nicer to wear than that."

Jillian laughed out loud as I gave our British friend the fiercest scowl that I could.

"If your airline hadn't lost that particular piece of my luggage, then I wouldn't be so stressed about finding something appropriate to wear. I blame you people."

Lestrade took off his jacket, loosened his tie, and sat down on the bed. "Go. I told you where to look. You're meeting Her Majesty the Queen tomorrow morning. Try to make yourself presentable."

"Hmmph. Sherlock? Watson? You two will be

on your best behavior. No barking, no pooping, and Watson? No farting, all right?"

Both corgis ignored me. They jumped up onto the bed, settled on either side of our British friend, and turned to face the wall-mounted television. Then, both turned—expectantly—to Lestrade, who returned their frank stare before laughing and reaching for the remote.

Jillian took my arm. "Let's go, Zachary. They'll be fine."

"I can't believe we have to go clothes shopping here in London," I complained, as we headed outside the hotel's front entrance and flagged down a taxi.

"Please take us to the nearest John Banks clothing store," Jillian instructed, as we clambered inside the black cab. "And stop your fretting. The outfit you were planning on wearing isn't here. Unless you'd like to give Americans a bad name, we need to make sure you're properly attired."

"Fine. You win."

Forty-five minutes later, we were inside the clothing store, browsing through rack after rack of various types of attire. Shirts, pants, and jackets. That was the only thing on my mind, and since a quick glance at the colors on this particular rack showed there was nothing I'd be willing to wear, I was ready to move to the next rack.

Jillian's slender hand snagged my arm and held me tight as I passed. "What do you think about this one?"

The shirt was dark green, which was fine. It had long sleeves, which I detested, but I did recognize the importance of the current situation. In this case, I'd bite my tongue. A long-sleeved shirt would be fine. But, the fabric itself? It looked and felt like a flippin' napkin, the kind you'd find inside a bag with an order of fries.

"The fabric feels terrible," I decided.

"Oh, it can't be that bad. Let me feel it. Oooh, you're right. It's horrible. Moving on. Instead of looking at every single rack, why don't you look for something you like?"

Sighing, I moved several racks over. There was a selection of business shirts that didn't look half bad. Selecting a dark navy blue shirt (long-sleeved again), and verifying it was the right size, I held it up to Jillian.

"What do you think about this one? It looks nice, doesn't it?"

"It does, yes. And it fits?"

"It's the right size," I insisted, as I checked the tag a second time. For the record, it didn't. The neck size was much too small.

Nearly an hour later, we were still shopping. While not ideal, I did manage to find something that was semi-sorta formal: black wool trousers, a pair of Oxfords, and a shirt that continued to make me cringe, namely a blue shirt with white pinstripes, complete with white buttons.

"I look like a mobster," I had complained, after trying on the shirt Jillian had found.

"Does it fit?"

"Yes."

"Then, it'll do. This is a once-in-a-lifetime opportunity. We are *not* going to mess this up."

I sighed. "Yes, dear."

"I see some dinner jackets over there. Stay right here. I'll go see if I can find one that will fit."

"Yes, dear."

Now, I know what you people are probably thinking: Jillian has me on a short leash. Well, it may seem that way, but trust me, my fiancée is only looking out for my well-being. If a beautiful woman wants to help you do something, especially when it falls into a category that you are admittedly not good at, you'd be a fool not to accept the help. Jillian knew what I needed to get, and she knew what I would enjoy wearing. I could only trust her.

Watching her wander off, presumably on a course for whatever rack she had spotted, I caught sight of something that had me gasping with alarm. A dark figure ... wait. Let me rephrase. A figure wearing a dark outfit had just ducked behind the closest rack of clothes. There was something about his demeanor which had me flagging down the first clerk I could see.

"Hey, do me a favor, would you?"

"Of course," the middle-aged woman, wearing the equivalent of a tuxedo, said. "What can I do for you?"

"I think you had better call for some security. I

just spotted someone duck behind that rack over there, and this was after my fiancée headed in that direction."

"At once, sir."

A loud commotion sounded nearby. The individual, having overheard every word I said (which was the plan, by the way), bolted from his hiding place and made for the door, but not before snagging his sleeve on the rack that had been concealing him. It went down with a large crash, which only spurred the darkly-clothed stranger to run that much faster. A few moments later, he made it to the store's front doors and dashed through just as they opened to admit several new customers.

"What's going on here?" a gruff, female voice demanded.

I hooked a thumb at the door as I turned to see a tall, blonde woman wearing khakis and a bright red shirt. There, festooned across the woman's back, was the word *security*.

"Did you see the guy who just sprinted out of here?"

"I did, yes. What of him? Did he steal something?"

"No, but I did catch him following my fiancée. She headed that way, toward the cashier you see there, when I saw this guy crouched behind the rack that is now tipped over."

The woman immediately reached for a radio and relayed several commands. It was at this time

Jillian wandered back, holding a suit jacket still on its hanger.

"What happened?"

"We had a tail. I saw him watching you as you walked away. He ducked behind the rack when he saw me, and when I asked for security, here tore out of here as though his... well, as though his rear was on fire."

"Did he knock over the rack?"

"Yes." I noticed several employees trying to right the overturned rack and lent a hand. "Here, I'll grab this part, you grab that part and you, grab the bottom and hold it steady."

Together, the three of us pulled the rack upright. Jillian brushed by me and pointed at something on an open hook on the rack.

"Was he wearing black?"

"Yes. I know he hooked his clothing in the rush to get away. Do you see a sample?"

Overhearing, the blonde security lady crowded close.

"Yes, right there. From here, it looks like a type of nylon, or maybe vinyl."

"Don't touch it," the woman ordered. "We'll take it from here. Will you ... ma'am? By your right foot. Do you see that?"

The two of us inspected the ground. I pointed at the folded piece of white paper partially under the rack.

"I think she's pointing at that. Looks like a folded-up picture to me."

"To me as well," the lady security officer said. "Would you?"

"Sure. Here, we'll kick it over, just in case."

"Perfect. Well, well. It would seem your supposition was right, Mr. …?"

"Anderson. Zack Anderson. This is my fiancée, Jillian Cooper. What is it? What do you have?"

The paper was unfolded and presented to me. What I was looking at was a grainy, shot-from-a-distance photograph of two very distinctive people, walking two very familiar dogs in an airport. Jillian was less than enthused.

"Zachary, your mystery person had our picture? How? Where was this taken?"

"It's recent," I decided. "Look. We don't have our luggage. That meant we had just arrived here, in London, and were on our way to the baggage claim."

"This doesn't make me feel good," Jillian whispered.

"The feeling is mutual. Come on, let's get out of here. I want to get back to the hotel."

"Are you worried about Sherlock and Watson?" Jillian asked. "We left them with a police detective. I'm sure they're fine. Besides, you're not leaving until you try this jacket on. Don't forget what we have to do tomorrow morning."

"Oh, come on. I've got slacks, shirt, and fancy shoes. Do I really need a jacket, too?"

"She's the Queen of England. What do you think is appropriate?"

Giving an exasperated sigh, I slipped the jacket on. I know what you're thinking. What business did I, someone who was about to meet the Queen, have in turning up my nose at a jacket? Well, the reason I don't like trying them on is because I can never find one that fits properly. If I try one that comfortably covers my torso, then it becomes super-tight around my chest. If I find one that fits properly around my chest, well, then the lower portion of the jacket would flare so much that I'm sure I could use it as a parachute. That's why Jillian had a jacket especially tailored for me. For the first time in my life, I had a jacket that fit comfortably, and didn't mind wearing on special occasions.

Then the good folks at London Heathrow Airport lost it.

"Hmm," Jillian tsked to herself. "Fits good in the chest area?"

"Yeah, but like all the other jackets I've ever tried on, this one, with the chest as large as it is, is designed for someone with a huge gut."

"You're the one built like a line-backer," Jillian teased.

"I know," I groaned. "That's why I *hate* shopping for clothes."

"Will this one work?" Jillian persisted. "It's the last thing we need to get for you."

"Yeah, it fits. Badly, but it fits. I suppose this one will do."

"Good. Come, let's finish up here and get going."

"Worried about the dogs, too?"

"Actually, I'd like to talk to Lestrade."

"You would? Why? To let him know about our stalker?"

"Well, yes, but what I'd really like to do is take him up on his offer."

"What offer was that?"

"To look up customs and traditions on the Internet," Jillian said, as I swatted away her credit card and presented my own. "You can buy the shirt and pants, but the shoes and jacket? They're on me."

Once we were in a cab and on our way back to the hotel, I found my mind jumping between two different subjects: our mystery person and the fact that, by this time tomorrow, we will have met Her Majesty the Queen. Did you hear that? I was going to meet the Queen! And why was that? Because my dogs could solve mysteries, and just so happened to solve a really old case that happened over a hundred years ago. Well, I should also mention that the Queen is a huge fan of corgis, and I know she'll enjoy meeting two more. It's just that … I never imagined I'd be in this position several years ago. After all, I was sitting next to my fiancée, talking about what we needed to do in order to *not* embarrass ourselves, and …

My mind trailed off as, turning in my seat to slide a few bags around so that I could sit closer to Jillian, I noticed we had picked up yet another shadow. This time, it was a black SUV with windows tinted so dark that it was impossible to see inside. Now, I will be the first to admit that I really had no way of knowing if this car was following us. For all I knew, the two of us could have been headed in the same direction. What made this particular car stand out, though, was the simple fact that they kept the same amount of distance between us, which was about three to four car lengths. If we slowed down, they slowed down. If we increased our speed to pass another car, they did the same.

Turning to look over at our driver, I slipped a twenty-pound note out from my wallet and slid it through the divider.

"Hey, would you do me a favor? Could you make an unexpected turn? Say, turn left at the next light?"

"What's that?" the driver asked, as he looked at me in the rear view mirror.

"What did you ask him to do?" Jillian asked, confused.

"Keep facing forward," I instructed, dropping my voice so that only she could hear me. "I think our friend is back. We're being followed."

"Really?" Jillian started to turn in her seat when I caught her arm and held it steady.

"No, don't look. I'm pretty sure these windows aren't tinted, and I don't want them knowing we're aware of their presence."

"We're being followed?" the cabbie repeated, having overheard our conversation.

"I think we are." I sighed. So much for keeping a

low profile. "Three cars back. See the black sedan?"

"Tinted windows?" the driver asked.

"That's the one."

"Oh, blimey. I've always wanted to do this."

"Don't do anything drastic," I ordered. "I just want to know if they're following us."

"You got it, bub."

The taxicab turned left and gently accelerated.

"You've got the mirrors," I told the cabbie. "Did he turn?"

"He surely did!" the driver exclaimed, growing excited. "Can I lose him now? I know I can do it!"

"Hold on. We have a friend at Scotland Yard. I want his take on this." Pulling out my phone, I dialed Lestrade. "Hey, amigo. How's it going?"

"How's *what* going?" Lestrade wanted to know. "Watching your dogs? The little darlings fell asleep watching *Queens of Mystery*. So, did you find …"

"Let me stop you right there," I interrupted. "I think we're being followed."

"And this isn't just another vehicle traveling in the same direction as you are?"

"I'm sure."

"Mm-hm. Allow me to venture a guess. It's a dark-colored car, with tinted windows, is it? And since the windows are so dark that you cannot see inside, they are—without a doubt—following you."

"It *is* a sedan," I confirmed, "and you're right about the windows. However, I had our cab driver take a different course and this car has turned to follow us each time."

There was a silence on the other end of the phone. This was apparently not what the detective sergeant was expecting to hear.

"Make and model? License number?"

"Can you tell what type of car it is?" I whispered to Jillian.

"I'm sorry, no. They all look alike."

"What about a hood ornament?" Lestrade pressed. "Distinctive features?"

"Well, I can see there's a white rectangle on the front grille," I said, as I turned to study the sedan. "Hey, could you slow down a little bit? I'd like to get closer to that car so we can see what type it is."

One would've thought I had just announced a family of ducks was trying to cross the road. The taxi came to a skidding halt, effectively relocating me from the back seat to one of the flip-down seats facing backward. I'm just glad the bottom portion of the seat had been folded down, or else I would have ended up crashing into the divider.

"Zachary! Are you all right?"

"I'm fine, I'm fine. Can you see that car?"

Jillian turned to look, but the instant she did, the black sedan sped by us and disappeared down a nearby alley.

"What's going on?" Lestrade wanted to know. "You didn't just get into an accident, did you?"

Painfully returning to my seat, I shook my head. "No, but our driver had a great time slamming on the brakes when asked to get closer to the car following us."

"Get a look at the manufacturer's emblem? Have a license number for me?"

"No, I'm sorry, I don't."

"I got a look at that emblem on the front grill," Jillian said, offering me a smile.

"I'm putting you on speaker," I told Lestrade. "Now, Jillian, tell us what you saw."

"It was a white rectangle, with a yellow bird on it. Both wings were raised, like it was about to take off. And tail feathers! It had some really long tail feathers."

"Could the bird have been golden instead of yellow?" Lestrade asked, keeping his voice neutral.

"Yes, I suppose so."

"Zack? Take your phone and look up the emblem for the Toyota Century."

Bemused, I did as asked. Once I had the picture on my display, I showed it to Jillian.

"That's it! Nicely done, Detective Sergeant!"

"Thank you, ma'am."

"What can you tell us about those cars?" I asked.

"They are a not-too-common automobile," Lestrade answered. "People do have them, don't get me wrong, but I can tell you that I mainly see them used on official business for various embassies."

"Excuse me?" I stammered.

"Oh my goodness!" Jillian exclaimed, at the same time.

"Zack, if what you say is true, then you were followed by representatives from another country."

"Is there any way we can tell which one?" I asked.

"We would if you were able to give me the first three digits in the license number. That two-digit code denotes which country the car is registered to."

"Figures. I didn't see it. Did you, Jillian?"

"I'm sorry, no."

"Hey, pal, by any chance did you?" I asked, turning to the driver.

"See the plate number?" the cabbie asked, as we locked eyes in his rearview mirror. "I didn't, no."

"Well, so much for that," I grumped.

The taxi suddenly swerved to the left, pulled into a small convenience store's parking lot, and came to a stop.

"What are we doing?" I asked, growing concerned.

The cabbie then touched his mirror. The rear view mirror then did the craziest thing: it lit up, showing me a video feed. I could only assume it was on this car somewhere. The cabbie tapped the mirror a second time, and the feed switched to a different one. In this case, I was now looking behind the taxi. My mouth fell open as I realized what the cabbie was doing. His car had dashcams and they had recorded the entire incident!

"New 4K cameras," the cabbie explained, as he tapped the display and accessed the stored video files. "They catch *everything*. That car of yours sped by us. That means it would've been picked up on camera. Ah, here we go. This was a few moments before you lot got in my cab. Fast forward a few moments and … yes! There it is. Let me see if there's a better shot of the license number. There we are!"

"Lestrade? Still with me?"

"Go ahead, Zack."

"I have a license number for you."

"Brilliant. Let's have it."

"Two five eight, space, the letter D, space, and then five-five-five."

"Two five eight?" Lestrade repeated. I couldn't see him, but somehow, I knew he was frowning. "Are you sure?"

In response, I snapped a picture of the still image on the mirror-display and sent it to Lestrade's phone.

"Did you just send me something?" Lestrade's voice suddenly asked.

"Yep. Go take a look, would you?"

"Hmm, well, I'll be buggered. You weren't kidding."

"What does that number tell you?"

"I'm checking right now to verify a few things. The first three digits are the country code. The letter D? It lets us know that this vehicle is restricted to London's city limits. And the final three numbers? That'll let us know who the car is assigned to."

"I'd like to know which country it belongs to," Jillian confided to me, in a low voice.

"The microphones on these cell phones pick up quite a bit," Lestrade chuckled, overhearing Jillian's comment. "I'm researching it right now. And … we have an answer. Huh. Wouldn't have called that one."

"Which country?" I asked.

"Kingdom," Lestrade corrected. "That number is registered to the Kingdom of Eswatini."

The two of us shared a look. Even the cab driver looked back at us, giving us a questioning look.

"Never heard of it," I confessed.

"Ever hear of Swaziland?" Lestrade asked.

"In passing," I said. "I really couldn't tell you anything about it. I don't think I could even tell you which continent it is on. What about you, my dear?"

"Sadly, I'm in the same boat as you are," Jillian confessed.

"The Kingdom of Eswatini is a land-locked country in Africa," Lestrade announced. "We English speakers will know it as Swaziland."

"Then, why not call it Swaziland?" I asked.

"Because," Jillian said, reading from her phone, "just a few years ago, the ruling king decided to officially change the name of his country to Kingdom of Eswatini."

"The Kingdom of Eswatini," I repeated. "Doesn't really roll off the tongue, does it?"

"It means Land of the Swazis," Jillian read. "Looks like the king has been calling his country that for a while and decided to make it official."

"And … did the king happen to tell anyone what his plans were?" I asked, stifling a laugh.

"I would think so," Jillian answered.

"How big is this country?" I asked.

"I was wondering that, too," Lestrade's voice chimed in.

"I'm checking," Jillian said, as she tapped and swiped her finger across the screen of her phone. "Here we go. Hmm, the country is about the size of Kuwait."

"Ah," Lestrade's voice said, pleased.

I gave my fiancée a helpless look. "That might help *him*, but that doesn't help *me*."

"Hold on. All right. It's a little smaller than New Jersey."

"Okay, that I can relate to."

"It says here that the Kingdom of Eswatini is a developing country and has a lower-middle income economy."

"I'm starting to think that someone is setting up this tiny little African kingdom," I chuckled. "A small, land-locked country in Africa was following us? Anyone else find that hard to believe?"

"I'm checking to see if any of Swaziland's cars have been reported stolen," Lestrade reported. "I'll call you back when I have something to report."

"We'll probably see you first," I told our friend. "We're on our way back to the hotel."

By the time we made it back to the Conrad London St. James Hotel, it was nearly forty-five minutes later. Traffic had been snarled both directions, resulting in a stop-and-go mess that had me eyeing the meter in the taxi every ten seconds. Jillian had to eventually sink her nails into my hand to keep me from scowling.

Walking into the room drew us both up short. There was Lestrade, shoes off, and jacket draped over a chair, resting on the bed with his back against the headboard. The corgis were lying on either side of him, out cold. From his upside-down position, Sherlock cracked an eye open and watched me for a few moments before returning to his doggie daydreams.

"I'm guessing they weren't a problem," I said, as I set my bag of purchases down on the desk.

"Not at all. I can see why the Queen is enamored of the breed."

I caught sight of something sitting just inside the door and groaned aloud. I nudged my fiancée and pointed at the item. Jillian burst out laughing.

"Zachary, look! They found your missing luggage!"

EIGHT

The following morning, the two of us were nervously waiting outside our hotel for our car to arrive. Thankfully, instead of having to wear the poorly fitting jacket I had purchased, I was able to look my best.

Waiting outside in the bright sunshine, I could only thank my lucky stars that it wasn't too warm out. Yet. I could already feel my internal thermometer climbing, but Jillian assured me that I was just being dramatic. Having always shied away from anything with long sleeves, unless there was snow on the ground, the simple act of me wearing a jacket was almost unheard of. In this instance, I was wearing my black custom jacket, a long-sleeved black business shirt, and black slacks. Yes, it looked like I was wearing an all-black tuxedo, but I rather liked the look, and having dressed in this outfit one other time, Jillian had assured me it was incredibly tasteful and very elegant.

I sighed as I wiped my brow with one of the tissues I had procured from our room. It might be elegant, but hoo-boy, was it warm.

Jillian was wearing a sleek black business suit, consisting of a black blazer, a black-and-white checkered blouse, and black skirt, which ended just above her knees. I had taken one look at her in her outfit and asked her, point-blank, how she had known to bring that particular outfit. I've seen Jillian's closet. I know full well that her wardrobe is extensive, and has an entire wall of her closet filled with professional-looking attire. Me? My fancy duds fit in one garment bag, and that is kept in the back corner of my closet. Jillian told me, after we both emerged, decked out in our finest, that she had peeked in my closet to see what I was planning on wearing. Knowing that I wasn't about to go out and purchase new clothes for this excursion, she had planned her own outfit around mine.

Do you see why I love her so much?

A dark red Bentley pulled into our hotel's loading area and came to a stop. Having been warned—by Lestrade—that the Queen would be sending one of her personal limousines to pick us up, and that it would be a dark maroon, I knew without a doubt this car was for us as soon as we saw it slowing near the hotel's entrance. I was in the process of stepping forward, to reach for the passenger door handle, when I felt Jillian pull me to a stop.

"Formalities must be observed," she whispered in my ear. "Let the chauffeur open the doors. It's his job."

Everything about this car screamed high price tags. I looked down at Sherlock and Watson and eyed the driver. "I don't know, pal. This car looks super fancy. Are you sure you want two dogs in there?"

"Super fancy?" the driver repeated, in what I insist was a mocking tone. He opened the passenger door and motioned for us to enter. "That is one way to classify it. There are only two of these cars in existence, and both were made for Her Majesty the Queen's Golden Jubilee."

"This is one of only two that were ever made?" I asked. "Er, dare I ask how much …?"

"The cars are valued at nearly ten million Euros each, sir. But, as you are no doubt aware, Her Majesty the Queen has owned dogs for most of her life. This will not be the first time a corgi has graced this automobile. Now, would these two be the delightful Sherlock and Watson I've heard so much about?"

Looking down at the dogs, I noticed both of them watching the driver with sheer adoration in their eyes. Moments later, both dropped to the ground and rolled over. I had to snap my fingers a few times to get their attention.

"Your royal canineships? Your coach has arrived. Would you like to board now?"

The chauffeur snickered and gave each of the dogs a thorough scratching.

"Pay no attention to your Yank. Do you want to

get pampered? You're in the right place, boys."

I pointed at Watson. "She's a girl."

"Sherlock is a girl?" the driver stammered.

"Sherlock is the tri-colored corgi. The red and white is Watson, and Watson is a *she*."

"Watson is no proper name for such a lovely lass as yourself," the driver crooned, eliciting a giggle from Jillian. "Come on, love. Let me give you a hand."

Climbing inside the luxurious car, I could only watch, bemused, as the driver reverently picked up each corgi and set them inside the car. Sherlock and Watson both turned to the driver and wriggled with delight.

"Brown nosers," I mock-grumbled. Jillian swatted my arm.

"You know our names," Jillian said, as the driver climbed behind the wheel. "What do we call you?"

"You may call me Mr. Tibbet."

"Very well, Mr. Tibbet," Jillian returned. "You know us, and now you know the dogs. How long will it take to make it to the palace?"

"Less than five minutes. Is everyone seated? Wonderful."

I didn't even feel the car move. It looked like the entire world was moving around me, and I was the one who was stationary. That's how smooth a ride that Bentley was.

"Zachary, look!"

Lost in my own thoughts, I looked up in time to see us pass through a gate and into the grounds for the palace. I could see the royal guards, decked out in their full-dress uniforms of red tunics and bearskins. One was slowly marching along the perimeter on the left, and I saw one doing the same going the opposite direction on the right.

"Looks like we have a welcoming party," Jillian observed, as the Bentley coasted to a stop several moments later. Mr. Tibbet had been right. The ride lasted all of about three minutes. "Then again, I only see one man looking directly at us."

"That is the Queen's private secretary," Mr. Tibbet reported. "He'll brief you on what to expect, where to stand, and so on."

As we exited the car, I lingered by the driver and offered my hand. "Thanks, pal. We appreciate the lift."

A faint smile appeared on Tibbet's face. "You're more than welcome."

"Would these two be the famous Sherlock and Watson?" I heard a male voice ask.

Turning, I saw both corgis sitting dutifully in front of a middle-aged man wearing a pressed blue suit. He peered through his black-framed glasses at the two dogs gazing up at him before giving them each a smile. Looking over at us, he extended a hand.

"David Xander, private secretary to Her Majesty the Queen, at your service."

I shook David's hand. "Zack Anderson. This is my fiancée, Jillian Cooper. And these two? Sherlock and Watson. Thanks for having us! Umm, I'm hoping you can tell us what we need to do, 'cause meeting royalty? That's a first for us."

"And what to expect," Jillian added.

"First time visiting our country?" David inquired, as he turned and held out an arm, indicating we should head toward an open double-door directly in front of us.

"Actually, no," I admitted, as I glanced down at the dogs. "But, I will say this is the first time that either of us have come here with the intention of looking around."

"I see. Right through there. Now, follow me please. We have to go through security, so I hope you don't mind."

"We don't," Jillian assured our new friend.

"Place all your metal objects in this bowl," a middle-aged man, wearing a dark blue suit, instructed.

"Can I ask where we're going?" I asked, as we headed deeper into the palace.

David turned to regard me with an unreadable expression. "You are here to meet Her Majesty the Queen."

I sighed. No sense of humor here. Then again, what did I expect? I was in Buckingham Palace!

"No, er, sorry. I know that part. What part of the palace are we going to?"

"Oh, my mistake. I'm taking you to one of the Queen's private chambers. She'll be with us in just a bit."

"I can only imagine how many audiences she

has granted in all her years as Queen," Jillian said.

David nodded. "It's less than you suggest, but more than you think. Here we are. Now, if you will allow me to offer some advice."

"Not only will we allow it," I began, "but we both openly encourage it. Neither of us want to make any mistakes in here."

David smiled warmly at us. "Trust me, neither of you have anything to worry about. Now, when Her Majesty the Queen arrives, I'd like to point out that there is no obligatory code of conduct. Her Majesty doesn't expect people to bow before her, but many choose to honor the traditional customs. That will be left to you."

"Got it," I said, nodding.

"If you choose to bow," David continued, "then it'll be just a subtle dip of the head. For women, a small curtsy."

"What about a handshake?" I asked.

"If Her Majesty offers first, then by all means. The thing to remember is, don't overdo it."

I looked at my fiancée and offered her what I hoped was a reassuring smile. "I think we can handle this."

"I hope she goes for a handshake first," Jillian confessed.

"Not able to curtsy?" I asked.

"Not well," Jillian admitted. "Think about it. There isn't much use for curtsying back in Pomme Valley."

"Anything else we should know?" I asked, eager

for more advice.

David nodded. "Actually, yes. Tradition dictates you shouldn't speak until Her Majesty has a chance to speak first. Allow her to say the first words."

"How do we address her?" Jillian wanted to know.

"The correct form to address her, for the first time," David explained, "is *Your Majesty*. Any subsequent reference after that would be to simply refer to her as *ma'am*."

"Ma'am," I repeated. "I can handle that."

"I heard two distinct syllables," David said, as he looked at me. "Just one. Ma'am, pronounced the same as *jam*."

"Ma'am," I said, trying again. "Thanks. See? That's the type of goof we're looking to avoid."

"Avoid personal questions," David continued. "Don't ask about members of the royal family in the media. Don't bring up any gossip you may or may not have heard." Responding to some unseen, or unheard, signal, David looked up. "All right, she's on her way. I will leave you two alone to ..."

An ear-splitting bark caused all of us to jump. Shaking my head, and letting out a deliberately louder-than-normal sigh, I looked down at Sherlock.

"That was loud, pal. Try not to do that for our next guest, okay?"

"My ears are ringing," David chuckled.

"Mine are bleeding," I remarked. "Sorry 'bout that. Sherlock doesn't like to be ignored. You said *two*, not *four*."

"You're telling me he barked because I ignored him?"

"The number of his quirks seem to be growing on a daily basis," I laughed.

"Good luck, you *four*," David told us, as he headed for the door.

Puzzled by the comment, I turned to look back in the direction where David had departed, intent on asking for some clarification, only standing there in his place was Queen Elizabeth II. The ninety-plus-year-old monarch had her hands clasped behind her back and was smiling at the two of us. I should clarify. She was staring at two of our little group, and it certainly wasn't me or Jillian. Sherlock and Watson were both wriggling with delight but were currently sitting. Seeing how they had yet to be given permission to greet the newest arrival, the corgis were acting as though they had sat upon a nest of fire ants, and were anxious to get moving.

"Good morning!" the Queen said, giving us a wide smile. "Welcome to Buckingham Palace."

"Hello!" I said, returning the smile. The Queen approached and held out a hand. Stepping forward, I took her hand in mine. This was someone in their nineties? Her grip was surprisingly firm. I could only hope I had half the strength she had when I was that age. "I'm Zachary Anderson, Your Majesty. This is my fiancée, Jillian Cooper."

Jillian performed a very small curtsy, which

earned her a huge smile from the Queen. "I'm so very honored to meet you, Your Majesty."

"The pleasure is all mine," she returned. Then, we watched her gaze drop until she was looking at the corgis. "Would this be the Sherlock and Watson I've heard so much about?"

By now, both dogs were squirming like crazy, but thankfully, neither had budged an inch toward the English monarch. The Queen was all smiles as she looked at the two corgis.

"Yes, ma'am," I confirmed, making darn certain I said the word as David had instructed.

"How delightful! Now, if I'm not mistaken, one is male, and the other female?"

I pointed at the closest corgi to her. "That one, the one with the tri-color coat, is Sherlock. He's male. The other one is Watson and yes, she's female."

Certain I was going to get some good-natured ribbing, she surprised me by holding out a hand. When neither dog moved, the Queen of England looked up at me with an expectant look. Sighing, I shook my head.

"Are you sure, ma'am? Those little boog … I mean, those two are quite energetic, and they absolutely love meeting new people. Perhaps you should be sitting down?"

"Nonsense. You may release them. I would love to greet them in person."

"Does this place still have dungeons?" I whispered to Jillian, as I stooped to unclip the leashes.

"If he does what I think he's gonna do, then ..."

"Oh, just trust them to behave themselves," Jillian returned.

"Guys? You're on your best behavior, is that understood? No jumping, no drooling, and Watson? No f ... no ... you know what I mean. Don't even think of it, girl." Looking up at the Queen a final time, just to triple check she was okay with what I was about to do, I unclipped the corgis' leashes and stepped away. "All right, you two ... *release!*"

Sherlock and Watson scrambled across the tile floor, each in a mad effort to be the first one to make it to the Queen. Her Majesty eyed the two approaching corgis, smiled, and held up a wrinkled hand. Shocking me senseless, the two galloping furballs instantly hit the brakes, which allowed them to spin themselves around until they were facing me. They then slid the remaining few feet to arrive by her side.

Sherlock looked up at the reigning Queen of England and nuzzled her leg. Watson saw her reaching a hand down and gave it a friendly lick.

"Oh, my, they are delightful, aren't they?"

"I know it, they know it, and everyone else knows it, too," I confirmed, between chuckles. "Thank you very much for inviting us. It's a real honor to be here."

"When word reaches my ear of a corgi pair, appropriately named Sherlock and Watson, solving the mystery of the missing Irish jewels," the Queen said, as she moved to a nearby chair and sat down, "then I simply must find a way to show my gratitude. Personally."

I looked at Jillian and shrugged. Of the many conversations the two of us have had regarding this very meeting, being given some type of reward for the return of something that clearly didn't belong to either of us had never been considered. The Queen wanted to reward us?

"You gave us free tickets to come see England," I returned. "That, in itself, is all the thanks we need. We appreciate your generosity."

"Generosity?" the Queen repeated. Her smile was back on her face. "I haven't even begun, Mr. Anderson. Ms. Cooper?"

"Oh, no, I'm fine," Jillian assured her. "You don't need to give me anything. I have everything I need, right here."

The Queen's eyes twinkled with merriment. "Is that so? I thought for certain you would be asking about your brother, my dear girl. My apologies. Heavens, what was I thinking?"

The dogs fell silent, as if both corgis had just been instructed to be as silent as possible. Jillian gasped with surprise, and I couldn't help but admire the Queen. Here she was, as old as she was, and yet she was sharp as a tack, warm and approachable, and clearly had a sense of humor.

"Er, what do you know about Joshua Cooper?" I asked.

"Well, I *am* in a position to know a thing or two,

young man," the Queen told me. "Please, sit. Let's talk about it."

"We really didn't come here to discuss my brother," Jillian insisted.

"Oh, but you did," the Queen insisted. "First Lieutenant Joshua Cooper, stationed out of Manassas, Virginia, has been closely working with our MI6, I believe, in the locating and recovery of stolen historical artifacts."

"Like a certain silver chest," I said, more to myself than anyone.

"Exactly," the Queen said, pleased.

"Do you know what he was working on when he disappeared?" Jillian asked, as she dropped her voice to match mine.

The Queen nodded. "I believe he was searching for someone. Several people, in fact. If memory serves, and it certainly isn't what it used to be, it was something about sisters."

"The Twins," I said, nodding. "That matches up with what we found in his notebook."

A look of surprise appeared on the Queen's face. "Notebook? I wasn't aware of a notebook. The Metropolitan Police searched all the various rooms he used and came up empty-handed, I'm afraid."

"The Metropolitan Police?" I repeated, confused. "What happened to Scotland Yard?"

"Scotland Yard refers to a branch of the police, called the Criminal Investigation Department," the Queen explained. "And Scotland Yard? The public entrance to the police station was affectionately named Scotland Yard, due to the original station being located on a street by the same name."

"I did not know that," I admitted, giving the Queen a smile.

"Nor did I," Jillian added.

"About this notebook," the Queen said, fixing her eyes on Jillian, "where was it procured?"

"We found it at our hotel," I explained. "Well, let's be honest. The dogs directed us to the front desk, and from there, we asked if there was anything left in Joshua's room."

"The Lost and Found department," the Queen said, shaking her head. "And you say Sherlock and Watson alerted you to its presence?"

I nodded. "It's hard to explain how they work. Whenever we're working a case, and the dogs show signs of interest in anything, then I'll usually take a couple of pictures, which will make no sense at that time. It won't be until much later that, upon reviewing those pictures, we'll see what the dogs were paying attention to."

"How did you know your dogs wanted you to check with the staff at the counter?" the Queen asked.

"They turn into a team of Clydesdales and physically pull me, like they're pulling a plow, to whatever they want us to see."

"They pulled you to the front counter," the Queen said, nodding, turning her attention to the dogs. "How delightfully clever. There is something I have been wondering about."

"What's that, ma'am?" I wanted to know.

"It's one thing for the dogs to indicate where you should be, or what you should be looking at, but how does that work for something like that silver chest? I'm told it was a type of puzzle box. How did your wonderful dogs help you solve it?"

"They didn't help," I clarified, "but, instead, they *solved* it. Of all the symbols and designs on all sides of that chest, the corgis let us know which ones we needed to be looking at. Sherlock would come up to the box and touch his nose on the piece that we needed to focus on. And, for the record, they got it right each and every time."

"Simply amazing," the Queen breathed. "I've always thought the breed was intelligent. This confirms it."

"Could I ask a few more questions about my brother?" Jillian asked, hopeful.

The Queen nodded. "Of course, my dear. What …?"

Her Royal Majesty the Queen trailed off as an aide suddenly appeared, holding a sheaf of papers. After the Queen gave an imperceptible nod of her head, the aide hurried to the Queen's side and whispered something in her ear.

"I'm terribly sorry," the Queen began, as she rose to her feet. "It would seem I need to take a phone call. Would you be so kind as to wait here? I'll be right back."

"Of course," I said, nodding.

If only she would have waited another twenty

seconds. I'm not talking about the Queen, nor am I talking about Jillian. No, I'm sorry to say, I'm talking about Watson. Those familiar with my little female will know that she sometimes has ... digestive distress. In layman's terms, Watson will occasionally eat too fast, something I'm desperately trying to help her overcome, and as a result, inadvertently swallow air. What's the result?

Watson let one rip. A loud, high-pitched hissing noise, reminiscent of a trickle of air being released from an inflated balloon, or else someone releasing the hydraulic brake of a semi, sounded noisily by my left foot. Surprised, shocked, horrified, and darn it, amused, I looked down at Watson, who was busy watching her packmate.

"Oh, come on, Watson," I whispered. "Really? You have to do that here?"

A titter of laughter sounded from behind us. Bemused, Jillian and I turned to look. There was the Queen, who had her hand on the doorknob, pausing to look back at us. She was smiling and her eyes were twinkling with merriment. Oh, that's just great. Watson farted in the presence of the Queen, and Her Royal Majesty the Queen heard her.

"We are *never* going to be invited back here," I groaned, once we were alone.

Jillian fanned the air. "My, that's a ripe one. One would think you feed her vegetables on a daily basis."

"Why does it always smell like rotten broccoli?"

I asked, as I covered my nose. "Wow, does anyone have a match? Can we open a window?"

"There aren't any in here," Jillian informed me. "It'll be fine."

"It'll be fine? I think my eyes have melted. Watson, I sure do hope that's the only one."

Just then, a second wave of stench hit us. A clear image of a rotting carcass of an animal, sweltering under a hot African sun, suddenly sprang to mind. Waving a hand in front of my face, I looked down at my sweet, timid girl. What had happened? Well, that was easy. Watson had doubled down, by releasing one of her infamous silent bombs.

"Holy moley, I need to check something." Gently picking up my red and white girl, I verified what I was smelling was only gas, which it was. "Good. No poo. Watson? Do you have an upset tummy, girl? Did you get into something you shouldn't have?"

The sound of a door opening behind me confirmed the Queen was back. I was also certain there was no way that foul stench could have dissipated in time, so I had no idea how she was going to respond.

"Did you know I've had corgis since I was fourteen years old? I named my first little girl Willow. I miss her every day. She used to have a similar problem."

"And what problem would that be?" I asked, genuinely curious.

"She would eat too fast and end up flatulating.

Quite often at the most inopportune time, too."

I felt my face redden. "I am so sorry about that. I have no idea why Watson eats so fast. She's done that ever since I adopted her. Harry, my veterinarian friend from back home, claims that it should've passed with time. I guess not."

"Do not hold it against this lovely girl," the Queen ordered. "She cannot help it."

I held out a hand, indicating my two dogs. "I wouldn't dream of it. Believe it or not, these are my first two dogs, ever. Oh, I've been around dogs before, don't get me wrong, but these are the first two I've ever been directly responsible for. And do you know what? I can't imagine my life without them." I placed my hand over Jillian's. "Or her, for that matter."

"How wonderful," the Queen said, smiling. "Have you picked a date for your wedding yet?"

"Well, no, we were waiting for ..." I trailed off as I realized the subject of my and Jillian's wedding was of a private nature, and only discussed among friends. How in the world did she find out about it? "You definitely have the advantage," I chuckled. "There's only one thing stopping the two of us from officially getting married."

"Locating your brother," the Queen guessed, as she nodded. "Perhaps I could help?"

"You already have," I argued. "You've given us a direction to go: Twin Sisters. We have a pretty good idea what it refers to, only we have yet to figure out how Joshua fits into the picture."

JEFFREY POOLE

"Then, you have deduced their nature," she said, nodding. "They are, in fact, cannons. Your state of Texas has apparently lost track of them, and your brother, my dear, managed to find them."

"I'm really not too surprised," Jillian admitted. "Joshua can be ... stubborn, so if he sets his mind to it, he won't let it go until he gets what he wants."

The Queen smiled at Jillian. "Indeed. Your brother, Ms. Cooper, was solely responsible for the recovery of those cannons. Your country should be proud."

"I know they're from Texas, and are a part of their history," Jillian began, "but if Joshua has returned something the locals call the Texas Holy Grail, how is it no one has heard of it?"

"Because they haven't been officially returned yet," she answered. "Give it time, child, and they will."

"What do you know about these cannons?" I asked.

"They were used by the Texas military forces during the Texas Revolution, or so I'm told," she continued. "They were very well known in that they were directly responsible for winning the battle of San Jacinto, in 1836 I think it was."

"How do you possibly remember all this stuff?" I asked, incredulous. "I mean, you have probably accumulated all kinds of facts and knowledge throughout your lifetime, haven't you?"

"Don't make too big of an issue out of it," the Queen told me, adding a conspiratorial tone to her voice. "These cannons? I only learned about them this morning."

"Wait, what?" I sputtered. "You assumed we'd be asking about Jillian's brother?"

"I *knew* she would be asking about her brother," the Queen corrected. "No assumptions were necessary. Besides, from what you've told me, I'm surprised Sherlock and Watson haven't indicated anything about what Lieutenant Cooper had recovered."

I thought back to the several instances when the dogs had seemingly stared at innocuous items, and I ended up taking pictures of everything. Well, the time to review those pictures was rapidly approaching, but it certainly wouldn't be proper to review them here, with the Queen. Good grief, what would my friends think back home if that did happen?

"Something tells me that they more than likely already have, isn't that right?" the Queen teased.

"Corgi clues," I murmured. I then went on to explain what they were and how they would always end up linking to the case we were working on in some fashion. "I just have to review them, ma'am. I'm sure I'll spot something in there which will confirm their royal highnesses, um, er, I'm so sorry. What I meant was, I'm sure Sherlock and Watson are well aware of the connection."

"Corgi clues. Excellent. Now, let me see if I can get you started on the right path to locate your missing family member." She then pressed something on her chair. Almost immediately, the nearest door opened and a female aide appeared.

"Yes, ma'am?"

"Do show Chief Inspector Warren in, please. Thank you."

"Chief Inspector Warren?" I repeated. "Is he someone who has seen Joshua?"

The door opened a second time, admitting a gentleman in his mid-sixties. He had a thick, white mustache and a head of curly graying hair. He hurried over to the three of us and stood stiffly at attention.

"Chief Inspector, this is Mr. Zachary Anderson, and Ms. Jillian Cooper. Ms. Cooper is the sister of Lieutenant Joshua Cooper. Would you kindly tell them what you discovered last night?"

Now, I need to pause here a moment and point something out. Those who are familiar with my dogs will more than likely have already noticed it. If not, let me point out that, during the introductions, a certain someone was left out, and that particular someone absolutely *hated* to be ignored. I had been so wrapped up with what the chief inspector was going to tell us that I didn't notice. Well, Sherlock didn't disappoint.

My little tri-colored corgi let out a bark that felt like it was strong enough to shake the dust off the chandelier in the room, not that it had any. That's just great. First, Watson does her best to clear the room of all living organisms, and now Sherlock takes it upon himself to rupture the eardrums of everyone present. Naturally, that included Her Majesty the Queen.

"I am so sorry," I began. "Sherlock doesn't like to be left out of introductions."

A knowing smile appeared on the Queen's face. She didn't say anything, but I could tell she was amused.

"Adorable dogs," Chief Inspector Warren observed.

I pointed at Sherlock. "Well, if you haven't lost your sense of hearing, that's Sherlock, and this one is Watson. They're helping us with a case."

"The detective dogs," Warren murmured, shaking his head. "Amazing. Are the stories about these two true?"

I nodded. "They've solved murders, located missing jewelry, and have even located missing people. They literally put our local police department to shame."

Warren smiled politely and pulled out a folded piece of paper from the inside of his suit jacket.

"We found a piece of property we suspect was owned by First Lieutenant Joshua Cooper. We were hoping you could confirm, Ms. Cooper?"

"I can try," Jillian said, taking my hand in hers. "It's been a while since I've seen any of his belongings, so I don't know...."

"One worn leather haversack, and on the inside, there's a patch with ..."

Jillian's eyes widened and she gasped, "... with the Jolly Roger on it."

Warren nodded. "It would seem my supposition was right. There's a patch of this pirate flag on the bag. This haversack clearly belonged to Lieutenant Cooper. I have my boys going through it right now."

From the corner of my eye, I watched the Queen's head turn to regard Jillian for a few moments. Looking at my fiancée, I could see Jillian was close to breaking down completely. I wrapped an arm around her shoulders and held her tightly.

"We're going to find him. I promise."

"Chief Inspector," the Queen interjected, "you will see to it the bag is returned to Ms. Cooper."

"Once we're done processing it, ma'am, you have my word it will be given to …"

A slight frown appeared on Her Majesty's face.

"… back to the Cooper family with all haste. In fact, they've had that bag long enough. Let me make a phone call. I'll have that bag, and all its contents, returned to you …"

The Queen gave a little cough.

"… before you leave Buckingham Palace," Warren quickly amended. "If you'll excuse me?"

"Of course, Chief Inspector. And thank you for your help."

The act of Chief Inspector Warren exiting the chamber, namely hearing a door close in the distance, caused both corgis to fire off warning woofs.

"Take it easy, guys. This isn't your house. There's no harm done, all right? So, take it down a notch. I don't need either of you to … Sherlock?

Not on your life, pal. Don't even think about taking that glove. Do you hear me? No! Put it down! Your furry little butt is going to get into trouble!"

The Queen, it would seem, had placed a pair of gloves she had been holding on a small white, circular table that was within arm's reach. However, her aim had been just a tiny bit off, and one of the gloves had been dangling, precariously, over the edge. Well, I don't know if there had been a sudden change in the air pressure, and it changed when Inspector Warren had left, but for whatever the reason, the glove dropped to the floor. Sherlock had noticed almost immediately, and had slowly inched over to it.

"I can still see you, you little snot. That is *not* for you. Drop it."

As you can probably imagine, Sherlock had other plans. He let out a playful *woof*, his head ducked low, and his short nub of a tail wiggled happily. I then made the mistake of taking a step toward him.

"Rrrrrrroof!" Sherlock challenged, his mouth full of glove.

The little snot took one look at me and bolted. What followed was nearly five minutes of me trying to act stern, and appear like I was supremely annoyed, only Sherlock was smart enough to know that I'd never get that angry with him. So, he kept just enough space between me and him and challenged me to get closer.

I heard a laugh come from behind me. Looking

back, I could see that the Queen was thoroughly enjoying herself. Her eyes were clear and bright, and were sparkling with humor. She watched Sherlock's antics for a few more moments when she finally held up a hand.

"That will be enough. Please return my glove, Sherlock."

My jaw hit the floor as Sherlock promptly trotted over to Her Majesty and spat the glove at her feet.

"You little brown-noser," I grumbled.

As our visit wrapped up and we bade farewell to the Queen, we were stopped dead in our tracks just as we were about to step out into the corridor and back to the front entrance.

"I do look forward to trying your wine, Mr. Anderson."

I turned to look back with a look of surprise written all over my face. Jillian and I shared a look. The Queen of England knew I owned a winery? Someone had done their homework!

"I'm honored, ma'am. I know my wine master sells the bottles online, but all you had to do was ask. I would have gladly sent you a bottle."

"We purchased several cases," she informed me. "It will be served at our next garden party. Good day to you all."

NINE

"A nd Caden thinks I don't try to promote the wine," I said, as we emerged from Buckingham Palace and back into the real world. "I wonder what he's going to think about that?"

"He is going to be beside himself once he learns that Lentari Cellars is going to have its wine served at one of the Queen's garden parties," Jillian remarked. "Zachary, would you do me a favor? Don't tell him until I'm there. That's something that I would love to see."

"Deal. Now that we have Joshua's backpack, why don't we …?"

"Haversack," Jillian interrupted. "It's a haversack, not a backpack."

"What's the difference?" I wanted to know.

Jillian held the bag up by its one and only strap. "Backpacks have two straps. This has one. It's designed to be worn over one shoulder."

"Did you see the Queen frown when that Warren fellow insinuated he wasn't ready to release the bag?" I asked.

"I did. There's a woman you do not want to cross."

"What do you expect? I mean, look how long she's been in power. There's a reason for that, you know."

Mr. Tibbet had been waiting for us, but after seeing firsthand how close our hotel was, we decided to simply walk back. After all, the four of us could do with a bit of exercise. Besides, we were both anxious to check out Joshua's bag.

We noticed a bus stop nearby, with a bench, and automatically headed toward it. Once there, and we claimed the bench for ourselves, Jillian decided to inspect her brother's haversack. Fumbling with the bronze buckle, she lifted the flap and peered inside.

"I don't suppose there's anything good in there," I said, as I leaned over her shoulder to take a look. Movement from the ground caught my attention. The corgis, it would seem, weren't interested in the slightest and both were settling themselves to the ground to watch the people wandering by. "Did we get anything good?"

"Just a change of clothes," Jillian reported, as she snaked her arm into the bag to explore the contents. "There's a mini-toiletry kit in here, too. Oh, wait. What's this?"

My fiancée pulled out a small, leather-bound

book. Having several of these myself, I knew immediately what it was: a hand-stitched journal. I do believe we might have finally caught a break!

"That looks promising."

"It's a journal, isn't it? Maybe it has … no, I think it's his personal journal." Look, there are multiple entries in here. Looks like he wrote in here several times a week."

"Anything good?" I asked.

"Not really. There's no mention of any cases he's working on, if that's what you're wondering. He talks about food, about the weather, and the traffic. Joshua, it would seem, was *not* a fan of driving in England."

"When was the last entry?" I wanted to know.

"From last Wednesday. It's just more of the same stuff. It … oh, here's something. Hmm, that's odd."

"What's it say?" I asked.

"Well, let's see. There's not much to it, just a few sentences. There's mention of his time in London, friendships he's made, and the sights he has seen. Here, see what you think."

Glancing down at the entry, I could see right away that it wasn't that long. Jillian had been right. This entry was less than a full page, but longer than a typical paragraph. Something about it struck me as strange.

HAVE ENJOYED YAMMERING TO WELL-WISHERS EVERYWHERE. ENJOYED TASTING IN-

TENSE EATABLES, CHECKING ROUND, OUTSIDE WINDSOR, NEAR MANY APPEALING RESTAURANTS. INSIDE NEW ESTABLISHMENTS, REALIZED I NEVER GAVE DEVILED BANGERS OR XIGUA CAKE HEED. SORRY, TAT.

Granted, it sounded strange, but it was more than that. I couldn't place my finger on it. Hoping there was something about the journal that would pique the dogs' interest, I held it down to Sherlock and Watson. Sherlock's ears immediately perked up as he sniffed it. Then, he nudged it a few times, almost dislodging the book from my hands.

"That settles it," I decided. "There's something about this journal. You're sure this is the only strange entry?"

"You're free to look for yourself. I didn't see anything else in there."

Flipping through the journal confirmed Jillian's observation. This unusual entry was the only one I found.

"Does it mean anything to you?" I asked, as I turned to Jillian.

"Have enjoyed yammering to well-wishers," Jillian read. "If I didn't know for certain this was Joshua's writing, I'd say someone else wrote this."

"I take it he doesn't talk like that," I guessed.

"No, he doesn't. Yammering? He doesn't use words like that. And he talks about trying different foods? Deviled bangers and xigua cake? That doesn't make any sense."

"All right, I'll bite. What is xigua cake? And don't tell me it's cake made from a xigua, whatever that is."

"Xigua is just another name for watermelon," Jillian said. "Xigua is its Chinese name."

"Watermelon cake? He's complaining that he didn't get to try a piece of watermelon cake? Why not just say that?"

Jillian fell silent as she studied the journal entry. After a few moments, she shook her head. "I'm sorry, I just have no idea why Joshua would write this. It makes no sense to me."

I heard a snort of exasperation. Glancing down, I saw that Sherlock was still watching me. Let me clarify. He was staring at the journal.

"There's no hidden flaps? No secret messages anywhere?"

Jillian ran her hands along the journal's outer leather cover. She gently pried and pulled various parts of the book before giving me a helpless look.

"If there is, then it escapes me. Why do you ask?"

Wordlessly, I pointed down, at Sherlock. By this time, though, Watson was mimicking her pack-mate, and both corgis were staring at the journal.

"Maybe something is written in invisible ink?" Jillian suggested.

I took the journal back and studied it. "Or, more likely, there's something up with this weird passage. Tasting intense eatables. It's a strange way to say he was sampling the local cuisine, don't you think?" My eyes were drawn to the last two words. "Sorry, tat. Tat? Think it could be short for someone's name?"

"If so, I have no idea who," Jillian returned.

"Sorry, tat," I repeated. Glancing at the third word from the end, I shook my head. "Heed. Then, Cake. I don't … wait. Cake, heed, sorry, tat. Well, I'll be a monkey's uncle."

"Do you see something?" Jillian asked, with the tiniest bit of hope in her voice. "Tell me you found something."

"Possibly. Look at the last four words and tell me what you see."

"Cake, heed, sorry, and tat."

For those of you wondering where I was going with this, look at the following, and tell me if anything stands out:

CAKE **H**EED. **S**ORRY, **T**AT.

See it now? CHST. Jillian said her brother used *chips have started tumbling* as a way to indicate things are going wrong. Was that why this passage sounded funky? Because it had a hidden message in it?

"Do you have a pen and paper with you, by any chance?" I asked.

It was then that I noticed Sherlock and Watson settle back to the ground. Amazing. I finally picked up on the fact there's a hidden message and now, with their job done, they can relax. I have absolutely no idea how they do it.

"It's the back of an envelope, but it should do," Jillian said, as she handed me the scrap of paper and a pen.

Double-checking the journal, I forced myself to only notice the first letter of each word.

HAVE **E**NJOYED **Y**AMMERING **T**O **W**ELL-WISHERS **E**VERYWHERE. **E**NJOYED **T**ASTING **IN**TENSE **E**ATABLES, **C**HECKING **R**OUND, **O**UTSIDE **W**INDSOR, **N**EAR **M**ANY **A**PPEALING **R**ESTAURANTS. **I**NSIDE **N**EW **E**STABLISHMENTS, **R**EALIZED **I** **N**EVER **G**AVE **D**EVILED **B**ANGERS **O**R **X**IGUA **C**AKE **H**EED. **S**ORRY, **T**AT.

Now, if you look closely, ignoring the second W from well-wishers, you'll notice we get the following letters:

HEYTWEETIECROWNMARINERINGD-BOXCHST

Add in some punctuation, and it becomes:

HEY, TWEETIE, CROWN, MARINE, RING, DBOX, CHST

"I have a question for you," I said, after I had finished jotting down the message. "Has your brother ever given you a nickname?"

"Several. Why?"

"Think hard. Has he ever called you Tweetie before?"

My fiancée gave me her answer before she could say a word. She gasped audibly and slapped a hand over her mouth.

"I've never told that to anyone. How did you know? Was that actually hidden in the message somewhere?"

I presented the scrap of paper to Jillian and tapped the decoded message. Her eyes filled as she read the seven word message. After a few moments, she looked up at me.

"I used to have this yellow hoodie when I was little," Jillian began, using a far-away voice. "I would wear it all the time, regardless of the weather. Hot, cold, rain, or snow, I'd always have my hoodie on."

I nodded. "Yellow sweatshirt, therefore, the Tweetie moniker."

"Exactly. Oh, Zachary. Joshua left this message for us!"

"You mean, he left it for you," I corrected.

Jillian ignored me. "Crown marine ring. He has to be referring to the ring he left for us to find at the Tower of London."

"That's exactly what I was thinking."

"And dbox? Short for Dropbox?"

"Again, that's what I was thinking. The problem there is, we've already found our way into his Dropbox account. It didn't have anything useful in there."

"What if ..." Jillian began, as she stood and started to pace. The dogs watched her intently from their positions on the ground. "What if that wasn't the account he kept all his files in?"

"Why wouldn't it be?" I countered. "We were able to access it, and we did so by finding—and using—the special Marine Corps ring we found with the Crown Jewels. You're suggesting there's a second account?"

"It'd be the perfect way to hide details you didn't want anyone else to discover," Jillian insisted.

"Well, all right, how do we determine what his login credentials would be?"

Jillian tapped the journal. "I think our answer is right here. Tweetie? Why call me that name, after all these years?"

"You said it was one of your nicknames," I recalled.

"Yes, from my childhood. I had to have been no older than eight or nine. We had plenty of names we called each other. Don't you find it curious that he'd choose to use a name that we literally haven't used in decades?"

"There's a reason for it," I guessed. "I can get on board with that. So, when you were known as Tweetie, what was Josh called? Sylvester?"

"Pepe," Jillian said, shaking her head. "Pepe Le Pew."

"The skunk? That's hysterical. And ... I don't want to know why."

"All the girls fawned over him," Jillian said, as she pulled out her phone. "Granted, it's not exactly like Pepe Le Pew, but I always called him that anyway."

She tapped the screen a few times before a familiar logon prompt appeared. Crossing my fingers, I watched Jillian type in the username and, when she made it to the password screen, looked up at me.

"What do you think? Same password as before?"

"Oh, man. I don't remember what it was before."

"Men," Jillian snorted. "All right, I'm typing in the password."

"For curiosity's sake, that would be …?"

"EN1GM@_THG_," Jillian answered.

The screen flashed angrily. The credentials had not been accepted. I pointed at the username.

"Doesn't the username have to be capitalized?"

"No. Username is rarely case-sensitive."

"Maybe it is in this case?" I suggested.

"It isn't. Hmm, I'm not sure where we go from here. I thought for certain we were on the right track."

I closed my eyes and thought of the letters hidden on Joshua's ring. How did we know if the order was right? The first part of that password, EN1GM@, was easy enough to decipher: enigma. What, however, did the THG refer to?

"THG," I softly muttered. "Did we ever figure out what it stood for?"

"I never figured it out," Jillian admitted. "Why?"

"We don't know which order the letters are supposed to be in," I said.

"Yes, we do," Jillian argued. "It worked for his other account, didn't it?"

"But, that doesn't mean that it'll work for *this* one, does it?"

"Oh, I see what you mean. Perhaps I should reverse it?"

Thinking hard, I shook my head. "That's the obvious choice. No, I think we should make the THG part first. It's what I would do if I was trying to protect a hidden account, but not make it too difficult to access."

Jillian's mouth dropped open. She anxiously returned to her phone and typed the new combination of letters and symbols into Dropbox's login page.

"Zachary, I'm in! Oh, my goodness! I'm in!"

"Very clever, Josh," I murmured. "Can't wait to meet you, pal. Just hang in there."

Jillian wrapped her arms around me and encompassed me in a hug. "I'm so worried about him."

"So, what's in the second account? Is there any way of telling?"

"Oh. Just a moment. Here. Zachary? It's all about those Texas cannons. He has detailed notes everywhere. Where he suspected they were hidden, where they were found, *when* they were found, and so on. Oh. Do you remember the LSS reference?"

"I do, yes. Should be a reference to Texas, right?"

"That is correct: Lone Star State."

"Hang on, I see another folder, and this one says Florentine."

"That's the name of a foreign city, isn't it?"

"Italy," Jillian confirmed. "Hmm, looks like Joshua was working on something for Florentine, although, I can't say what. Looks like it was a missing something-or-other, and whatever it is, it's yellow."

"Did he find it, too?"

Jillian shook her head. "Not yet, but he's mentioned several final resting places."

"What a job," I breathed, amazed. "Tracking down and locating lost relics. I think that's every guy's dream job."

"Is it yours?" Jillian asked.

"To be Indiana Jones? Oh, heck yeah!"

"I found something interesting about those cannons," Jillian reported.

"Fire away, dear. Er, pun intended."

"Mm-hmm. Anyway, we already know the cannons were located and recovered, don't we?"

"According to the Queen, yes. Do you see something about when they're going to be returned?"

"I don't, no."

I shrugged. "Well, if these cannons are as historically significant as he's made them out to be, then I'd like to think that they would have made the news."

"True. Maybe they're waiting for the right time?"

"No time like the present," I decided. "Why do

you bring this up?"

Jillian tapped her phone. "Well, if this happened, say, a week or two ago, then why are there all these new references to the Twin Sisters case?"

Leaning over my fiancée's shoulder, I read what I could see on her phone's display. The problem was, the text was incredibly tiny, and my eyes weren't *that* good. "New references? Can you give me an example?"

"This file has notes about suspected retaliation," Jillian read, after she opened the text document on her phone. "This folder has pictures of a house. A pretty house, mind you, but just a house."

"What about the house?" I asked, as I peered over Jillian's shoulder to see for myself. "Yeah, that's really cool. Looks kinda like a house I've seen on Lord of the Rings. Like ..."

"... a hobbit house," Jillian finished for me.

"Exactly. Look, the door even looks round, even though I'm pretty sure it's the surrounding hillside growing over the frame. Look at it! I love the way it looks like that particular hill has been hollowed out."

"Do you see the windows?" Jillian asked. "There's one here, here, and here. Whoever owns that house is a fan of Middle Earth." She switched folders and immediately tapped the screen. "Here's something for you."

"What do you have?"

"See this? It's a page of hand-written notes. I can tell, just by looking at it, that Joshua is the one who wrote it. Here, do you see what it says here? And here? I'll save you the time. Joshua has doodled all over this page. Zachary, stop laughing. Now, look what it says here. NO. It's written over here, too, and again over here. Joshua clearly believed the person who *had* the cannons was a member of our NO organization."

"No *what*?" I asked.

"No nothing. NO, as in Nameless Organization, remember?"

I snapped my fingers. "Got it. Joshua thinks that whoever stole these cannons is part of … of NO?"

"Depending on how sinister these people are," Jillian began, "then it's not hard to believe that they might be wanting to exact some retribution against my brother. Oh, look here. Here's DF again. And again, over here. Davis Forrester?"

"Your brother's friend? Didn't we determine that he and your brother knew each other?"

Jillian fell silent as she stared at the screen. After a few moments, her eyes widened and I could tell she just figured something out.

"What is it?" I asked, eager for some news.

"I just realized something. I think …"

"You think *what*?"

"I think it's not safe out here."

I hooked an arm through hers. "Come on. Let's go find some place safer than being out in the open. I'm curious as to what you found, but it can wait. I say we return to the hotel and see what we can figure out about who had been holding onto these cannons. If this was the last case Joshua worked, then there's a better than average chance there will be a clue or two in there that will indicate where he found them, and who had them in their possession. Sherlock? Watson? Are you guys awake? Come on. It's time to go."

A quick stop by one of the bus tour stands provided directions for the closest pick-up point for the public buses. With my arm companionably hooked through Jillian's, we waited for our ride to arrive. However, that's when I heard something that made my skin crawl.

"Woof."

Surprised, I looked down. Sherlock was looking off to the left at the mass of people strolling about. His hackles were raised, and the fur was standing up on his back. Based on the little corgi's body language, the devil himself must be walking among us, and was now inevitably headed our way.

"What's he barking at?" Jillian wanted to know.

"I'm not sure. There's nothing that way except, oh, I don't know, several thousand people?"

"Woof."

"Yeah, okay, I heard you pal. That really doesn't help us too much. Hmm, what say we go for a little walk?"

"What about the bus?" Jillian asked, perplexed.

"We'll either grab a taxi or look for the next bus stop."

"You think there's someone out there, don't you?"

"It's a possibility," I admitted. "I'd like to know for certain. Sherlock? Watson? Let's go for a walk."

You'd think there was a band of ninjas behind us, because every ten seconds or so, both dogs would slow down to turn their heads all the way around and look behind us.

"Guys! Knock it off! If there's someone back there, then the last thing we want to do is let them know *we know* they're back there, got it?"

Both corgis snorted once, in unison by the way, and promptly faced forward. At first, I thought they were mad at me for making them ignore who-ever, or whatever, was behind us, but I could also see that Sherlock's hackles were still raised. He hadn't let his guard down, which could only mean he was following orders! Seriously, are all dogs this smart? How could that little corgi know I wanted him to be less obvious than he was already behaving?

Dogs.

"How are we supposed to tell if someone is following us?" Jillian whispered to me.

"Well, I'd say the easiest way to see if we've picked up a shadow is to find a legitimate excuse to come to an abrupt stop, which, preferably, points us the other way. That way we can see if someone else abruptly stops, too."

"Do you have any ideas?" my fiancée asked.

Once more, the dogs took the decision-making process out of my hands. I had just passed a cast-iron lamp post on my right when both corgis decided to walk completely around the post. Since I can say I was distracted, I can also say that I didn't notice what they had done. So, problem solved. I was brought to an immediate and very unpleasant stop.

"You knuckleheads. What in the world did you do that for?" Realizing I knew *exactly* why the dogs did it, yet amazed at their grasp of the situation, I gave both dogs a grin before making a huge play on getting the leashes untangled. "Now, look what you've done. You looped around … no, that's not an order. Sherlock? Stop moving, dude. Watson? Stay there, would you? Jillian, take Watson's leash. I'm going to unclip her and get her untangled."

While I carefully worked to unravel the mess the leashes had become, I was afforded the opportunity to look behind me. Sure enough, about twenty feet back, I could see a guy dressed in dark clothing, wearing a black baseball cap and sunglasses, pretending to look at the menu of a sidewalk café. The entire time I pretended to be working on untangling the dogs' leashes, I kept an eye on the guy.

This stranger, whoever it was, kept throwing furtive looks my way while he held his ground at the restaurant's display. After a few moments, I held the leashes aloft in a victorious display of man defeating an inanimate object. While I was doing so, I turned around, so my back was to our unknown shadow, and I looked at Jillian.

"Send a message to Lestrade, would you? I'd personally like to figure out who this guy is, and who he works for."

Jillian held up her phone. "I'm way ahead of you. I've already apprised him of the situation."

"And?"

"And I'm waiting for a response. Here we go. All right, first off, is this the A3214?"

"You're asking me if that's the name of the road we're on? Hold on. Let me … yeah, that's right. You can see the street sign over there. Why?"

"Follow me, would you?"

I nodded. "Sure. Can you tell me where we're going?"

"You'll see. Is Sherlock still growling? Do we still have our tail?"

Catching sight of our mystery person's reflection in several store windows, I nodded. "He's still back there, and he just fell into step behind us. How far are we going?"

My fiancée pointed at the intersection we were approaching and indicated a shop with a bright blue façade. "We're going right over there. Doesn't that look delightful?"

"That's a shade of blue that I personally wouldn't have chosen to put on a pub," I decided, as I gazed at the sign for Bag O'Nails, a bar advertising itself as a traditional pub. But, much to my surprise, we wandered right by it.

"Umm, I thought you wanted to go inside and check it out?" I sputtered, completely lost.

"Wait for it," Jillian said, as she allowed her gaze

to fall on a window display several doors down from the bar.

Just then, no fewer than ten police officers rushed out of the Bag O'Nails and swarmed over the guy tailing us. Before I could even let out an exclamation of surprise, the guy was cuffed and forced into a sitting position on the street's curb. Lestrade, sporting the biggest smile I have ever seen on a person's face, approached.

"Is this the guy?"

"That's him," Jillian confirmed.

"Well, well," Lestrade said, as he squatted next to our mystery man, "what might your name be?"

"Go to hell," the man snarled.

"You first, chum. Now, let's see if you've got any identification on you."

The man was pulled to his feet and searched. Unfortunately, the only thing he was carrying was a smart phone. Lestrade tapped the device and then frowned when a security alert appeared and prompted him for an access code.

"I don't suppose you'd care to unlock this for us, or at least tell us what the code is, would you?"

The stranger's nose lifted, and his answer became clear.

"We'll get our boys at New Scotland Yard on it," Lestrade told us. "I'm sure they can find a way into these things."

I looked at the phone. "It looks like an Apple. Is it an iPhone?"

Lestrade rotated the phone in his hands and

then gazed at the logo visible beneath the transparent case. "Let me guess. This is the bloody model of phone that's unhackable, isn't it?"

I heard a couple of soft snorts. Looking down, I saw that both dogs were staring at the phone, as though I was holding an iPhone-shaped doggie biscuit. Sherlock then broke eye contact to look at our mystery friend. That's when a realization dawned.

"Do you mind if I try?" I asked, as I held out a hand.

Lestrade shrugged and passed me the phone. "Do you think you can figure out his passcode?"

"Probably not. Besides, these phones have safety protocols in place so that, if you guess incorrectly enough times, the phone will brick itself."

"It'll *what*?" Lestrade asked, confused.

"It'll lock itself up so tight that, in essence, it becomes as useful as a brick."

"Ah. That's just swell."

A smirk appeared on the phone's owner's face.

"But," I continued, "what do you want to bet he was foolish enough to set up an alternate way to get into his phone?"

"Like what?" Lestrade wanted to know. "A fingerprint?"

The stranger began to struggle. Oh, he knew I was on the right track, all right.

"Face ID," I reported. I held the phone up in front of our new friend, only he was struggling like crazy to keep his face away from the phone.

"We really don't have permission to do that," Lestrade said, correctly guessing what I was trying to do. "And, aren't you a police consultant? You really shouldn't be doing it, either."

The stranger stopped struggling and the smirk was back.

"But, I'm not," Jillian declared, taking the phone from my hand.

Before the incarcerated man could figure out what she was doing, Jillian held the phone directly in front of him, allowing the sophisticated device a full three seconds to look at his face. It was more than enough.

The phone beeped once and then the home screen was revealed.

"You have no right to do that," the man snapped.

"I'm not a police officer," Jillian smoothly returned. "So, let's see what's on here. Oh, I think you'll want to see this, D.S. Lestrade. His texts? Look at the last one, sent less than an hour ago. Oh, my. That's a good likeness of the two of us, Zachary, don't you think?"

"He had our pictures?" I asked, as I leaned over Jillian's shoulder to get a good look at the phone. "Imagine that. And, for the record, this is why I'm not a fan of biometric security. If you plug your mug into your phone, then anyone can unlock it just by holding it up to your face."

"That's assuming your phone falls into someone else's hands," Jillian added.

"True. Hey, what's that one say? The text message from earlier this morning? Could you open that one?"

"Sure."

"Put that down at once!" the stranger demanded.

Ignoring the suspect's outbursts, Lestrade crowded close as we opened up the second-to-the-last text. This one had my blood running cold. Jillian gasped with alarm and almost dropped the phone.

"*What's the price?*" I read, as I scowled at the phone's owner. "And the response? *Bounty claimed. Collection to be Saturday, noon.* Does that, or does that not, sound like Josh had a bounty on his head?"

"And, as expected, Lieutenant Cooper is being held against his will," Lestrade added.

"We don't have much time," I said, as I pointed at the phone. "They say that collection is taking place Saturday. That's tomorrow! That means we gotta find him, and we gotta do it *fast!*"

"But, how do we do that?" Lestrade protested. "We have no idea who's holding him."

I looked down at the dogs. Both Sherlock and Watson were watching me.

"The cannons. Whoever had those cannons must be holding a grudge against Joshua. If we can identify who that is, then we should be able to find Josh, only ..."

"Only what?" Jillian asked.

"We have to find him by the following day. Joshua is out of time!"

TEN

"Corgi clues? That's what you call these pictures? Oh, is that because these are photographs of what Sherlock and Watson wanted you to see?"

"That's exactly right," I confirmed, as I watched my phone circle around our table.

It was less than an hour after the confrontation on the street, and the three of us—humans, that is—were seated around a table at the Blue Boar Pub, here at the hotel. The dogs were back in the room, if you were wondering. We were trying to find something to let them watch on television when we found a rugby match between Wales and Ireland that seemed to attract the dogs' attention. Each of them would fire off warning woofs every time the players came together for one of their scrums.

"So, what are we looking at?" Lestrade wanted

to know.

The phone made it back to my hands. Gazing at the picture, I grunted. "This would be the very first photo I took. And, if memory serves, this shot and the one directly following it were taken of the bell-hop's hands after we arrived via taxicab."

"Why did you take a picture of his hands?" Jillian wanted to know.

"Why don't you ask the dogs? They were the ones staring at the guy's hands."

Jillian produced several sheets of paper. Selecting one, she grabbed her purse and pulled out a pen. "All right. Picture one. Hands. What about the hands? Anyone?"

I held the phone up close to my face. Jillian sighed and shook her head. "Buy Zachary glasses."

Lestrade let out a snicker.

"Please," I scoffed. "My eyes are fine. Now, what about the hands? Well, there's a small mole on the left hand. There's a gold band on the ring finger. I'm guessing it's either engagement or wedding related. Umm, the tip of the middle finger has a band-aid on it, like the nail has been hurt."

Jillian nodded. "Got it. What else?"

I flipped to the second picture. "Second verse, same as the first. Moving on. All right, here we are. This is a picture of Allyson, the girl from the front desk." Passing the phone to Lestrade, I shrugged. "I don't think this one is too hard to figure out. Allyson was manning the front desk. The dogs wanted us to ask about the Lost and Found department. It's where we found the notebook."

"So, why are the three pictures you took of the girl?" Lestrade asked, unable to disguise the mirth in his voice. "She looks a little young for you, doesn't she?"

Jillian managed to snag the phone before I could reclaim it.

"He's right, Zachary. If Sherlock and Watson wanted us to be focusing on the front desk, then they'd be looking at the front desk. Instead, they are looking at the girl."

"Can you tell why?" I asked. It felt like my face was on fire. Lestrade looked my way and grinned. "There's gotta be a reason why I took her picture."

"Well, she *is* cute," Jillian decided. "Zachary, I'm surprised. I didn't think you'd go for that type, being ..."

"All right, all right," I laughed, as I snatched away my phone. "We'll be deleting those pictures, thank you very much. Wait. Dear, look at her hands!"

"There are rings on every single finger," Jillian observed. She looked down at her notes. "The bell-hop also had a ring."

"You're thinking the connection to the rings is Josh's marine ring," I guessed.

"Right. Okay, moving on. Zachary? What's next?"

"Let's see. Next up we have ... a pool sign? What the heck did I take this for?"

"What is it?" Jillian asked, taking the phone.

"It's a sign for the hotel pool's hours. Did the dogs stop to look at this, or did you snap its picture accidentally?"

"No, I remember now," I said, shaking my head. "We had just stepped off the elevator when the dogs pulled me to a stop at that sign. They wouldn't leave until I took a picture of it." I swiped my finger to the left. "Make that two pictures. Pools. All right, people, who has any theories on what the dogs were trying to tell us about pools? Anyone?"

I was met with silence.

"Roger that, no one knows. Moving on. Okay, this one is easy enough. It's a picture of Joshua's ring, right after we got it out from the Crown Jewels exhibit at the Tower of London. We already know this ring held a secret, and that secret was the password. Does anyone have anything else they want to add?"

"As you said, that one is pretty self-explanatory," Jillian reminded me.

"I thought you said this was going to be difficult?" Lestrade said. "So far, we have, what, maybe one or two pictures that are unknowns? All the others seem to be perfectly relevant to the case."

I glanced at the next picture and then triumphantly held out my phone. "Oh, yeah? What about this one? This is the nice lady who sold me a couple of Pepsis in front of the hotel, if memory serves. What do you think the dogs were focusing on in this picture?"

Lestrade took my phone and stared at the display for so long that the phone threatened to power itself off. Giving the screen an irritable tap, our British friend finally shrugged and passed the phone to Jillian.

"I'm sorry, I haven't a clue. I think I might've spoken too soon?"

"This is who you bought my Pepsis from?" Jillian asked. "Why would the dogs be interested in that?"

"Can you see any rings?" I asked.

"No."

"What about cannons, or anything pertaining to the great state of Texas?" I asked.

Jillian was silent as she studied my phone. "No, I'm sorry."

"Let's approach it from this angle," Lestrade said. "What do you see, ma'am? What stands out to you?"

"Well, the woman is astride one of those street vendor carts. You know, half cart, half bicycle. Hmm, I should write that down. The bike is red, if that means anything. The company logo is visible on the cart part of the bicycle."

"And what is the logo?" I asked.

"It looks like a Chinese dragon, riding a bike."

"Dragon on a bike," I repeated. "I'm not sure how that helps us."

"That makes two of us," Lestrade confessed.

"Moving on," I said, raising my voice, "what do you have next, my dear?"

"I have a picture of moving supplies," Jillian reported. "I think this was when we had stopped at one of those tour bus kiosks. Am I right?"

I took my phone back. "Yeah, that's right. Sherlock and Watson stopped to stare up at the many pamphlets that were there. What is it, an advertisement for a moving company?"

Jillian expanded the picture on my phone's display and nodded. "I do believe that's exactly what it is."

"How does that help us?" Lestrade asked.

I stared at the picture of the boxes, moving tape, and the hand cart that was visible on the screen. "Well, there's … wait a moment. Boxes? Could the dogs have wanted us to look at boxes?"

"Why?" Lestrade wanted to know. "Why would they care if we were looking at boxes?"

"Dropbox," Jillian said, in a soft voice. "As in, Dropbox accounts!"

Shaking my head, as I blew a kiss at her, I checked the next picture, only that was it. I had hit the end.

"That's all there are," I said, as I turned to my two companions. "Ideas?"

Jillian held out her hand. "Could I have your phone? I'd like to run through the pictures one more time."

"Sure. Hope you can spot something we missed." While Jillian perused the corgi clues, I looked at my future wife and sighed. "Everything I can see leads us back to the cannons. Yes, from what you have told me, they were recovered. We still don't have any names to work with. Hey, wait a minute. Jillian, back before we strolled by the local London police hangout, and got rid of our latest tail, you were about to tell me what you had discovered in that second Dropbox account. Well, I don't think we could get any safer than we are right now. Care to share?"

"I've been replaying that episode in my head," Jillian confessed. "I don't know if this is something we need to investigate, and I don't even know it's true. And no, I didn't see any links in the second Dropbox account, but seeing his initials so often did make me think of it."

"Whose initials?" Lestrade asked.

"Davis Forrester," I guessed.

Jillian nodded. "Right. Zachary? What if Davis Forrester and my brother were not as close as we had thought? What if … what if this Davis person is the one who had stolen the cannons? What if he's the one who was in possession of the cannons in the first place?"

"What about the picture?" I reminded my fiancée. "We found that picture of the two of them, together. Wouldn't that suggest that they were friends? It certainly looked like they were in the marines together."

Lestrade pulled out his phone. "Should be easy enough to verify. Give me a few minutes."

"This is going to be weird if Davis is the person we've been searching for," I said.

"He's dead," Jillian reminded me. "If he *is* the person who had the cannons in his possession, then who killed him? Was it this Nameless Organization we keep stumbling across?"

"Cryptex Solutions," I said, snapping my fingers. "The high-tech storage facility. We might not be able to search it, but I wonder if we could find out if Davis Forrester had an account there? Wouldn't that confirm our suspicions?"

"Who do you think he's calling now?" Jillian asked, lowering her voice.

"I wish I knew. I think the last one was to his superiors. I heard him asking about Cryptex Solutions, so I figure he overheard us. What this one is about, I don't know. It has to be significant in some fashion, seeing how both dogs are now watching him like a hawk."

Ten minutes later, we had our answer. Kinda. Lestrade had been able to work his magic on his bosses, and they, in turn, looked into the military connection between Joshua and Davis. Turns out, I was right. They were *not* friends. Far from it. The two of them had gone at each other no fewer than five times, according to their company's CO. Oil and water, we were told.

"I'd say that confirms Davis Forrester's involvement," I said, feeling pleased.

"It doesn't answer who killed him," Lestrade reminded me. "No one I talk to seems to have any clue. Besides, don't believe everything you read."

"I'm surprised they didn't accuse Joshua," Jillian said.

"According to their commanding officer," Lestrade read, consulting his notes, "that was their first thought, only at no time were there any reports of Lieutenant Cooper starting the fights. In fact, even when he was provoked, he refused to lay a hand on his fellow marine. Said it was against the code."

I looked up. "Code? What code?"

"It's something to do with the marines," Jillian informed me, "and the code of living they adhere to."

"Ah, got it. So, Joshua had every reason to want Davis dead, or off his back, but from the sounds of it, he couldn't be provoked."

"Exactly," Lestrade said, nodding. The detective sergeant's phone chose that time to start ringing. "Lestrade here. Yes, sir, er, ma'am, I was just informing the ... what's that? We have access? You're kidding. How the bloody hell did that happen? Never mind, I don't care. May I ask what we found out?" The D.S.'s notebook appeared in his hand. "Yes, ma'am. That's pretty much what we were able to infer. Yes, ma'am. Yes, ma'am. What's that? No, ma'am, they're here. All of them. I will inform them at once. As for the list, could you email it to me? I'll check from my phone. Thank you, ma'am. Oh, I will, ma'am."

The call ended.

"That was a whole lot of ma'ams," I chuckled. Remembering the last person I addressed by that title, I felt the blood drain from my face. "Did the Queen just call you on your cell?"

Lestrade snorted with surprise and gave me a resounding *no*.

"Of course not. That was actually the Commissioner of Police of the Metropolis."

"Sounds like someone with power," I said, giving Lestrade a friendly nudge. When neither the nudge nor the smile was returned, I could only swallow nervously. "Is there anything we need to be concerned about?"

"Actually," Lestrade said, as he appeared to rouse himself, "I think we might have caught a break. I telephoned earlier, requesting confirmation that one Davis Forrester was a paying client of Cryptex Solutions, and I was immediately met with resistance. Well, the commissioner tells me that someone with more authority than she reached out to CS and just like that, they started cooperating."

"That's fantastic!" Jillian exclaimed.

"Yes and no," Lestrade said. "They're only confirming that Davis Forrester had a unit there, and that the account had been paid up for the next twenty years."

"Oh, wow," I whistled. "That couldn't have been cheap."

"For a place like Cryptex?" Lestrade said, frowning. "You're looking at a price tag with two commas in it, easily."

"How does a soldier afford an amount like

that?" Jillian asked.

"He wouldn't," I decided, as I looked at Lestrade. "Can we possibly find out who paid for Davis Forrester's unit?"

"I'm on it," Lestrade said, as he pulled his phone back out. "Let's just hope CS is still cooperating."

While Lestrade outlined what information we were requesting, I took Jillian's hand in my own and gave it a squeeze. "How are you holding up?"

"It feels like we're closing in on Joshua. I just don't know if I can handle what we'll eventually find."

"Don't think along those lines. Joshua is a resourceful guy. I'm sure he's going to be fine."

"If Davis was the one who had those cannons," Jillian began, between sniffles, "then would that suggest it was Joshua who confiscated them from him? I just don't understand who could've killed this Davis person."

"What about the person who paid all that money to allow Davis to have a unit at Cryptex Solutions?"

"Do you think they'll cooperate and give us this person's name?" Jillian asked.

"I sure hope so. I wonder why they're being so nice all of a sudden."

Jillian smiled. "What do you want to bet the Queen had a hand in this. Cryptex Solutions may want to keep their clientele private, but I'm also certain they'll want to stay in business here in the UK. Her Royal Majesty had to have a hand in clearing the way."

"Oh, it was Her Majesty, all right," Lestrade confirmed, as he finished his latest call. "Get this. Commissioner Edwards was actually on the phone with the CEO of Cryptex Solutions, who is, conveniently enough, based in Switzerland, when there came an immediate reversal of attitude. The CEO informed our commissioner that he had an incoming call, and when he returned, he offered to verify whether or not Davis Forrester held an account there."

"I'd love to hear how that particular conversation played out," I said, grinning, and rubbing my hands together in proper super-villain style. "So, we have confirmation. That's beautiful. Now, what about who paid the bill? Do we know?"

Lestrade nodded. "According to Cryptex, the account was paid by another account holder, Sergeant Major Miles Cavanaugh."

"Never heard of him," I said.

Lestrade looked at Jillian. "Ma'am?"

"I haven't, either. Why do you ask?"

"Because, ma'am, Miles Cavanaugh is ... *was* your brother's unit leader."

Jillian looked at me. "Is that a bad thing?"

"It's unethical," Lestrade announced. "Former commanders paying over seven hundred thousand pounds to rent a storage unit at a high-tech compound? For twenty years?"

"Do we know when the account was paid?" Jillian asked.

"Do we know how the cannons were recovered?" I asked, moments later.

Lestrade pointed at Jillian. "You first. The answer is yes, we do. It happened not long ago, nearly two months."

"And what about how the cannons were recovered?" I asked.

"All they would tell me is that Lieutenant Cooper intercepted a shipment intended for Cryptex Solutions."

A notion occurred. "This Major Cavanaugh ..." I began.

"Sergeant Major Cavanaugh," Lestrade corrected. "Retired."

"Right. Sergeant Major Cavanaugh. We know he has a unit at Cryptex Solutions, too, right?"

"That's right," Lestrade confirmed.

"How many?" I asked.

Lestrade looked up. "What?"

"How many storage units? Or, if it's just the one, how big is it?"

Lestrade nodded. "You think that maybe these cannons were originally held by Cavanaugh, and he sold them to Forrester?"

"That's exactly what I'm thinking."

"I can try to find out. I'll be right back."

"We're done here. Meet us up at our room, okay? I want to check on the dogs."

Lestrade nodded. "See you there."

"You're up to something," Jillian accused, once Lestrade had wandered off and we rose to our feet.

"What are you thinking?"

"Hear me out," I said, as we rode the elevator to our floor. "This Cavanaugh person has holdings in Cryptex Solutions. He knows they won't ever disclose what he's holding, and it was only by the authority of Her Majesty the Queen did the CEO start cooperating. So, what I'm thinking is, Cavanaugh had the cannons." Arriving at our door, we unlocked it to find both dogs stretched out on the bed, still awake, and still watching television. "You two are spoiled rotten. Now, as I was saying, for whatever reason, Cavanaugh decides to give the cannons to Forrester. Maybe the authorities were breathing down his neck? Maybe Forrester offered a hefty sum? For whatever reason, ownership passed to Forrester. I don't know how Cryptex would handle transfers from one owner to the other, so I could only assume it ..."

There was a knock on the door.

"We have a problem," Lestrade announced, as he hurried into the room. "Sergeant Major Cavanaugh did, indeed, have a unit at Cryptex Solutions."

"And the bad news?" I prompted.

"It was the smallest one they offer, at four feet by four feet. Do you know what that means?"

"The cannons couldn't possibly have come from Cavanaugh," Jillian deduced.

"Exactly," Lestrade praised.

"Well, so much for that theory," I grumped.

Lestrade held up a finger. "But wait, there's

more!"

Bemused, I took Jillian's hand and, together, the two of us sat on the edge of the bed.

"Hit us with your best," I said. "What's up?"

"Do you remember me mentioning Sergeant Major Cavanaugh was retired?"

We both wordlessly nodded.

"Turns out, a former American has moved to South Wales and is currently living like a king."

"Former American, living abroad, and living like a king," I repeated. "That's not suspicious at all. Do we know where in Wales?"

"We don't, I'm afraid."

"Do you have a map of Wales?" Jillian asked. "A large one might be easier than looking on our phones.

Lestrade nodded. "I do in my car, ma'am. Give me a few minutes, if you please."

"Wales might not be that big," I began, "but can we say *needle in a haystack*?"

"I think you'll see this might be easier than you think."

I watched my fiancée's eyes flick over to the dogs. Sherlock and Watson were both laying, Sphinx-like, and staring at the screen with wide, unblinking eyes. What was the program? Well, the rugby match was gone and now there was something about birds. Dogs.

So, Jillian thinks we might be able to figure out where to go in Wales? All right, color me intrigued. What did she know that I didn't? Hmm, better leave that question unanswered.

Lestrade returned, holding a folded map. He hurried over to the table and spread the map out. Lestrade and I turned, expectantly, to Jillian.

"Well? You're up, dear."

"Mm-hmm. Now, where's Cwmbran."

"Where's *what*?" I asked.

"Cwmbran. It's the little shipping office where Joshua mailed you that silver chest."

Lestrade and I leaned forward, looking for clues.

"Here it is," our British friend reported, tapping a tiny dot. "It's just north of Newport."

Jillian rose from her seat to get a closer look.

"Then, this is where we concentrate our efforts. I believe there are no surprises, and no coincidences. Joshua used the shipping facilities here, in Cwmbran, and I want to know why."

"You think there's a connection," Lestrade said. "Well, as you can see, there are no shortage of villages scattered throughout the area."

"Can you check to see the last known address of our friend, Mr. Cavanaugh, in Wales?" I asked.

"As a matter of fact, I have already put that request in. If they discover anything, or manage to locate an address, they'll let me know."

Fifteen minutes later, we had our answer, and once again, it caused the humans to gaze in open-mouthed astonishment at the two corgis.

"I've got something!" Lestrade announced, after hearing his cell phone beep an alert for an incoming text message.

"What do you have?" I asked.

"I have a last known address for one retired Sergeant Major Miles Cavanaugh. Well, I'll be…."

"What is it?" Jillian asked.

"Miles Cavanaugh lives in a little town by the name of … Pontypool, in Wales."

"Pool?" I repeated, glancing back at the dogs. "You're kidding."

"I'm not. I'm calling this in. Can someone check to see if there are any other villages in Wales with the word pool in it, just in case?"

"I'm on it," Jillian announced.

"Wait a moment," I murmured, drawing a look from my fiancée. "Wales? Refresh my memory, dear. What symbol is on the Welsh flag?"

Jillian's eyes widened. "A dragon! The dogs! They've been focusing on all things with a dragon on it. They've been telling us to focus on Wales all along!"

"That's impressive, guys," I softly told the corgis. I didn't want to wake them. Not yet, anyway. "You guys haven't lost your touch. Well, what about pool? Are there any other pools in Wales?"

"Well, it *does* look like there's another village with pool in the title: Welshpool."

I tapped the map. "Where is it? Is it closer to Cwmbran than this Pontypool place? Wow, that just doesn't roll off the tongue, does it?"

It took the two of us far longer than we would have expected, to locate the tiny town of Welshpool, Wales. And, it was nowhere near Cwmbran. Once Jillian found it, she let out an excited squeal.

"There we go! It's in the northern part of the country. That's at least, what, 140 kilometers away!"

I let out a sigh before I could stop myself.

Jillian shook her head. "Oh, I'm sorry. That works out to a little over ninety miles. Better?"

"Yes, thank you. So, does it seem like Pontypool is the right place?"

"It's enough for me," Lestrade said, grinning. "How would you fine folks like to go on a drive through the countryside?"

* * *

"I'm so very glad this trip has been sanctioned by New Scotland Yard," Jillian was saying, nearly two hours later.

We were traveling west, along a road simply called M4, heading toward the city of Newport. Travel time was estimated at three hours, and thus far, the five of us—including the dogs—were in high spirits. Knowing the corgis as well as I do, I fully expected to find Jillian's brother, more than likely held somewhere on Miles Cavanaugh's property. I know British cops don't typically carry weapons, but in this case, I actually noticed Lestrade packing some type of firearm in a shoulder holster.

"I absolutely love this country," Jillian said, taking my arm and giving it a squeeze. "The only thing missing is to see some round doors set into the hillside."

"Wales gets that a lot," Lestrade confirmed. "The Middle Earth analogy comes up quite frequently as tourists drive through the country."

"I'll bet their tourism industry doesn't complain," I joked.

"Not at all."

"What's your plan for when we arrive in Pontypool?" Jillian wanted to know.

Lestrade shrugged. "I am relying on your famous detectives to point us in the right direction."

I looked at the corgis, who were busy watching the passing countryside. "I hope they won't let you down."

"I know they won't."

A little over an hour later, we were heading northwest, having left the city of Newport behind us. According to the map, Pontypool was about ten miles north, while Cwmbran fell comfortably in the middle of the two. We did plan on stopping in the small village of Cwmbran, just to see for ourselves what the shipping office Joshua used to send me the silver chest looked like. But, a more pressing matter loomed over all of us: locating Joshua before he was turned in to the Welsh version of Jabba the Hutt.

Pontypool, I found out later, was a city of 28,000 residents. Driving through the small town, I was surprised at how big it actually was. Then again, the only city I can remember visiting in

Wales was Conwy, and it was about the size of Cwmbran: tiny.

Jillian had just nudged my shoulder and pointed at a dark green building. From the nearby signs, I could see that it was St. Matthew's Church.

"Look, how quaint! Can you imagine getting married there?"

"I thought we ruled out any type of religious ceremony?" I asked.

"True, but if the situation called for it, would you be amenable?"

"You mean, if the church was located in a cozy little village like this? Yeah, especially if it meant something to you."

My fiancée looked absolutely delighted. "Really? You would?"

"Provisionally so," I was quick to add. "The circumstances have to be right."

"I'll keep those in mind, Zachary."

"Woof."

The three of us, Lestrade included, turned to look at Sherlock. The corgis, I think I forgot to add, were sitting in the front left seat, which was what I normally thought of as the driver's seat, so that if something like this arose, Lestrade would be able to see them.

"What's it mean?" Lestrade asked, as he looked at me in the rearview mirror.

"I told you before, I don't speak corgi."

Jillian swatted my arm. "It means something has attracted Sherlock's attention. I think we might be getting close."

We drove on for another five minutes when we reached a fork in the road. Unsure which direction we were supposed to go, Lestrade started to turn in his seat, in order to ask us a question, when he saw the dogs. Sherlock and Watson were both looking to the right.

"Works for me," Lestrade muttered, as he hit the turn signal and turned right.

We proceeded for another few minutes before the dogs perked up again. There wasn't another fork in the road, but there *was* a turn coming up on the left. Sure enough, that's where the dogs were looking.

"Left it is," Lestrade said, turning left.

In this manner, following the directions the dogs chose to look, we headed out of town, following a course due northwest. Lestrade, who said he had been eyeing the odometer, claimed we were now about four miles outside of Pontypool city limits. That was when we almost ended up in the ditch.

"Awwwwwooooooo!" Sherlock suddenly howled.

"Oooooooo!" Watson agreed.

Lestrade jerked so violently that he inadvertently stepped on the brakes, which caused the car to fishtail across the road. Ten seconds later, the car came to a halt and every single one of us, I guarantee you, was wide awake.

"How about a little notice, pal?" I complained, as I released my seatbelt and massaged my sore chest.

"Where are we?" Jillian asked. She released her seat belt, too, and turned to look out her window. That's when I heard her gasp with surprise. "Zachary! Look! It's the house from the pictures!"

"What house and what pictures?" Lestrade demanded, as he peered at the house at the bottom of the hill.

"It's the hobbit house, all right," I confirmed. "Lestrade? I think we found what we're looking for."

ELEVEN

W hat if he's hurt? What if he's sick? What if we took too long to get to him and poor Joshua is … is …"

I pressed a fingertip against Jillian's lips. "Don't go down that road. Let's wait to hear what they find in there, all right?"

"I'm just so worried, Zachary. What if he isn't in there? What will we do?"

Watson whined and wiggled her way under Jillian's arm to snuggle against her chest. Jillian smiled appreciatively at the red and white corgi and held her tight.

"Thanks, Watson. I should trust you and Sherlock know what you're doing."

The two of us, along with the dogs, were still seated inside Lestrade's car. He, and what looked like the entire police force stationed in Wales, had disappeared inside the house currently registered to Miles Cavanaugh. A scant ten minutes after Lestrade radioed in his findings, nearly twenty-five patrol cars, each carrying at least three people, converged on the quiet house. Now, I know that our police departments back home, in the States, require a warrant to execute such a search. I imagine there's something similar in place here, only I don't know how long it takes to have one issued.

Here we sat, waiting for something to happen. I really wanted to see a procession of officers exit that house, with Joshua in the middle, so that my darling fiancée could finally stop her worrying. However, after a nerve-wracking thirty minutes of absolutely no news, and nothing to indicate how the search was going, I was about to exit the car and see for myself what was going on. However, Lestrade beat me to it. Our British friend had finally come outside. We saw him close the mostly circular door behind him, and head our way.

"Tell me you've found something," I said. "Tell me he's okay."

"There's nothing in there," Lestrade reported, looking as glum as he sounded. "We've checked everywhere, mate. There's no one in there being held against their will, I'm sorry to say."

"And you've looked everywhere?" Jillian asked. I could see her eyes beginning to fill.

"We've turned that place upside down," Lestrade confirmed.

"Has the owner been cooperative?"

Lestrade turned to point at a group of people standing nearly thirty feet away. One man in particular, wearing a tight black shirt, camouflage pants, and a pair of aviator sunglasses, stood out. He was graying, had his hair cut short, in a typical military buzz cut, and looked smug. Too smug, if you ask me.

"That's Cavanaugh right there," Lestrade said. "He maintains he has no idea what we're talking about, and insists he's innocent."

"Of course he does," I said, sighing. "Do you believe him?"

"Not a chance," Lestrade quickly responded. "He's hiding something. In this case, it must be your brother, ma'am. Wherever he's got him stashed, he knows we aren't going to be able to find him. And, unless we locate Lieutenant Cooper, then we can't charge Cavanaugh with a single thing."

"He's loving the attention," I decided, as I looked at the man with the angry, defiant expression on his face. "What I would do to be able to wipe that grin off his face." I heard the dogs whine. Turning to look at the corgis, a thought occurred. "I don't suppose you'd be willing to let Sherlock and Watson give it a try?"

"I was hoping you'd say that, Zack. Sherlock? Watson? Would you two be willing to help us?"

Both dogs reared up on their squat legs and pressed their noses against the glass, leaving twin streaks.

"I'll take that as a yes. Jillian? Wait here."

"What? No. I want to come with you."

"And if we find him and he's not in a position to be seen?" I countered.

"But ..."

"He's right, ma'am. You need to stay here."

"Come get me the moment you find something," Jillian instructed, wearing a frown.

"I will. Guys? Let's go."

As we were walking toward the front door, I could hear the homeowner's protests.

"Look, I've been more than considerate. You wanted to check my place out, and I've been more than accommodating. I tried to tell you there's nothing there, but you don't believe me. So ... what's this? I never gave permission to allow dogs in my home."

"You reside in Wales, under the jurisdiction of Her Majesty the Queen," one of the men said, as he puffed out his chest. "We are under orders, from Her Majesty, to use whatever means we deem necessary to bring this case to a close. If there's nothing in there, as you suggest, then you'll have nothing to worry about, isn't that right?"

"There's nothing there," Cavanaugh reiterated, through gritted teeth. "I think I'm going to call my lawyer."

"You're more than welcome to," the high-ranking official returned, as he turned to watch our procession approach the house.

"Does it look like Bilbo's house inside?" I asked, as the dogs and I stepped over the threshold and into the house.

I didn't need an answer. It was a definite *no*. For anyone who has seen any of the Middle Earth movies, they'll know that Bilbo's hobbit hole was the epitome of comfort. Big comfy chairs, inviting colors, and fresh scents of something baking in the oven. However, the appearance of a hobbit's residence was only a façade. Everything inside was as modern as one could get. Neutral, earthy colors, and no detailing. This room, and the others I could see, was simple and unadorned.

Definitely not my style.

I gave the leashes a gentle tug. "Sherlock? Watson? We're here. Joshua may be here, too. We need to find him, all right? Which way do you want to go?"

"Kitchen is that way," a nearby police officer told me, thinking I had asked his opinion. "Two bedrooms that way, and down the corridor opposite from us is the master bedroom. I don't know what you think you're going to find, sir, but we've checked 'em all."

Sherlock turned to look at the opposite hallway, gave himself a noisy shake, and then started off. With Watson trailing slightly behind, and me a few steps back, the three of us crossed the living room and stepped into the long hallways. The dogs ignored everything we passed, seemingly intent on making it to the end of the hall. The hallway extended another twenty feet before turning to the right and emerging into the vast master bedroom, which looked just as tasteless as the rest of the house.

In this room was something I had never seen before: an Alaskan king bed. Now, if you're curious as to what size that is, I encourage you to look it up. It is, single-handedly, the largest bed you'll ever lay eyes on. It made my California King bed look like a twin.

Measuring a whopping 108 by 108 inches, this bed was a full two feet longer than my California king bed, and nearly two and a half feet wider. Seriously, a bed this size would only work in the largest of rooms. Since this house was nowhere near spacious enough, a person's eyes were immediately drawn to the white elephant in the room. The icing on the cake was the frame the bed was sitting on, which raised it nearly three feet off the ground.

At the foot of the bed was a large cedar chest which, appropriately enough, looked miniscule next to this behemoth.

"Woof."

Surprised, I looked down at Sherlock, only he wasn't the one who barked. It was Watson, and she was staring at the chest. Sherlock, upon hearing Watson let out a soft woof, perked his ears up and then sniffed at the chest.

"Awwoooowooowooo."

"Three syllables," I reported. "You heard it here. There's something up with the chest."

"We've already looked inside," Lestrade was saying, as he reached down to open the chest. "See?

There's nothing there."

There wasn't a single thing inside: no blankets, pillows, sheets, or anything of the sort. Instead, it was as Lestrade had described: empty. I was about to tug on the leashes, to encourage the dogs to look elsewhere, when I noticed both corgis were sitting. Sherlock was staring at the chest, and Watson was staring at me.

Kneeling next to the dogs, I rapped my knuckles on the side of the chest. Nothing felt out of the ordinary, so why were the dogs so fixated on this thing? Straightening, I slowly spun in place, taking in the decorations, the knick-knacks, and the over-all décor of the room. A theory had just presented itself and I was curious to see if I was right.

I snapped a picture of the chest and sent it to Jillian, asking her to identify it. Within moments, she had responded.

IT'S A HOPE CHEST. TYPICALLY USED BY WOMEN. WHY?

Grunting once, I looked at Lestrade. "Mr. Cavanaugh. Can you confirm his marital status?"

"His marital status?" Lestrade repeated, confused. "He's single. He's a bachelor. You shouldn't be surprised by that. The man's a chauvinistic tosser."

I sent another message to Jillian, asking if it was unusual for a single man to have one.

IT'S HIGHLY UNUSUAL.

I pointed at the chest. "I think our answer is right there."

"It's just a storage chest. What about it?"

"I confirmed it with Jillian. This is a hope chest. Women use them to store things. Look around this room, pal. Do you see any other evidence of a woman living here?"

"I most certainly do not," Lestrade said, giving the room his own cursory inspection.

"There's this house, back home," I began, as I ran my hands along the side of the chest, "that was built during a time of our country's history where it was necessary to hide certain things from the authorities."

"Prohibition," Lestrade said, smiling.

"Exactly. This house had so many hidden rooms and compartments that I thought we'd never find them all. Care to take a guess as to who found the vast majority of them?"

Lestrade pointed at the corgis.

"Those two?"

"Precisely. They are quite good at locating hidden doors, compartments, and so on. So, I figure this is child's play. Besides, take a look at this." I nudged the chest with my toe. It refused to budge, as though it had been nailed to the floor. "It won't move. I think you'll find that it's attached to the floor in some fashion. Perhaps it's hiding something, like a false bottom?"

"By heavens, if it is, I'll find it. Hey, Constable.

Fetch me a hammer, would you? There's one in the boot of my car. And tell them to arrest Mr. Cavanaugh. I'm pretty sure he's not going to like what we're about to find."

Fifteen minutes later, it was all over. There was, indeed, a false bottom on the chest. Once Lestrade had broken through, a narrow staircase was revealed, leading down to a subterranean basement. There, sitting in one of three cells, with his hands bound and hooked to a chain which was drawn up over his head, was First Lieutenant Joshua Cooper, looking haggard, bruised, and underfed. As soon as Lieutenant Cooper locked eyes on me, and he noticed two wriggling corgis doing everything they could to escape my grasp to come say hello, a huge grin broke out on his face. He held up his zip-tied hands and, as soon as he was cut free, he hurried over.

"Zachary. At long last."

I shook Joshua's hand. "Nice to meet you, pal. Hey, listen, don't take this the wrong way but, you're a pain to track down, do you know that?"

As dire as his current condition was, Joshua threw back his head and laughed.

"Oh, is it good to get out of there. Now, who might these two be? Are they the famous Sherlock and Watson Jillian has told me so much about?"

Sherlock was beside himself. He wanted to come say hello, but I could also see that Jillian's brother was in no shape to receive a full-blown corgi welcome.

"Hang in there, guys. You'll get to give him a proper greeting soon. In the meantime, Joshua, I think you'll find someone outside that's been waiting to see you."

"Is Jillian here?" Joshua asked, amazed. "And call me Josh, would you? Only my sister calls me Joshua, Zachary."

"It's Zack, and you're on."

"Joshua!" Jillian cried, as soon as we all emerged into the sunshine.

I led the dogs away, intent on letting the two siblings get reunited with one another. Up ahead, on the right, I could see Miles Cavanaugh, with his hands cuffed behind him, being led away, his defiant smirk gone. In fact, he was completely silent as he was placed inside one of the patrol cars.

A paramedic arrived and pulled Josh to the side. Jillian followed the two of them over to the ambulance where my future brother-in-law was given a checkup. The cuts on his face were bandaged, a nasty laceration on his right hand was treated, and he was set free.

Jillian's arm immediately went through his.

"I'm so happy you're okay. You had me worried sick."

Josh turned to look at me and held out a hand. "Thanks for coming to get me. Both of you."

An ear-splitting bark made all three of us nearly jump out of our skins. Josh quickly squatted next to the dogs and ruffled each of their fur and then did something which surprised the heck out of me.

He planted a kiss on the top of each of the corgi's heads.

"You wonderful, brave dogs. I will never forget this."

The corgis, as you may imagine, writhed on the ground in pure ecstasy.

"Jillian? Zack? Can we go grab a bite to eat? It's on me."

* * *

The following day, the three of us were sharing our second meal together. No, it wasn't breakfast. None of us wanted to get up early, and that included the dogs. In fact, I had to rouse both of their Royal Canineships and get them outside to take care of their business. Sherlock and Watson were definitely not morning dogs.

While we were sitting at one of the Blue Boar's four tables on their tiny patio, waiting for our order to arrive, I looked at Josh and gave him a grin when he looked my way.

"What?" my brother-in-law asked.

"Now that you're here, I need to ask you something."

"Fire away, bro."

I had a quick flashback to Harry, my best friend back in PV. He always called everyone *bro*, too.

"Why did you send me that silver chest?"

"Because I knew you'd be able to figure out what to do with it," Josh smoothly returned.

"How?" I asked. "The two of us had never met,

and we hadn't ever talked. How could you have known that?"

Josh took a long drink from his beer and sat back in his chair. "They say if you really want to get to know an author, then all you have to do is read his books."

My eyebrows shot up. "You've read some of my books?"

"I've read *all* of your books. Once I heard my baby sister ..."

"Oh, don't call me that," Jillian groaned. I couldn't help but notice the smile *and* the blush on my fiancée's face.

"... had finally found someone else after she lost her first husband, I took it upon myself to make sure you were legit."

"And?" I prompted.

"Imagine my surprise when I discovered how much in common you had with Jillian. You two are perfect for each other. Now that I've answered your question, let me pose one of my own."

"Go ahead."

"Why the hell haven't you married my sister yet? Have you got rocks in your brain? Don't make me recant everything I just said about you."

Jillian and I both choked on our drinks, seeing how we had both reached for our glasses and taken a swallow at the same time. I grinned at Josh before looking over at Jillian. I placed a hand over hers and gave her a smile before turning back to Josh.

"Fine. You want to know why?"

"I'm all ears, Zack."

"It's because of you, pal."

"Me? What did I have to do with it?"

"You weren't here," I stated, using a tone of voice which indicated I wasn't going to apologize for taking this stance. "There was no way I was going to marry your sister until her family would be able to attend. *All* her family. You, pal, were always out of town, or more than likely, out of the country. So, we waited."

The bottle of beer Josh had been holding was slowly lowered to the table, a look of surprise etched all over his face.

"I ... I don't know what to say to that. Jillian, is this true?"

"Well ..."

"Come on, Tweetie. Tell me the truth."

For the second time, Jillian choked on her drink. Wiping her face with the napkin that I held out for her, she looked at her brother and shook her head.

"I was just telling Zachary that you haven't used that nickname on me in years. Now, in less than a week's time, I've heard it twice. For the record, don't call me Tweetie unless you want me to start using Pepe again."

"Deal," Josh said, grinning. "I am so impressed with how you handled everything. You figured out the clues, you found my ring ..."

"... and your notebook," I interrupted.

"What notebook?" Josh asked, frowning. "I didn't hide a notebook."

"The one in the hotel?" Jillian argued. "The same hotel we're staying at right now? Conrad London St. James? Housekeeping said they bumped the desk and that notebook fell to the ground."

Josh snorted with surprise. "Oh, *that* notebook. Wow. I had forgotten about that."

"You didn't want us to find it?" I asked.

"I didn't want *them* to find it," Josh corrected.

"Who? NO?"

"Nameless Organization," Josh laughed. "Sorry, I didn't know what else to call them. And yeah, them. I thought for certain I was being followed that day, and didn't know where else to hide it."

"What now?" Jillian asked. "Do you have to go back to work?"

Josh nodded. "Eventually. My boss did give me a four day leave, to rest and recuperate."

"Can you tell us what you're working on now?" I asked. "If you can't, just say so. No worries."

"Sure. You found my ring, so that means you found your way into my Dropbox account. And, I'm pretty sure you made it into the other one as well. So, you'll know that I'm adamant about keeping the world's treasures out of private hands. Historical artifacts belong in museums, not someone's study, or den."

"Couldn't agree more," I said. "Hey, can you tell us what iceberg and Coronado refer to?"

Josh nodded. "Iceberg. You've heard of the Florentine diamond?"

I hadn't, but Jillian had.

"The missing yellow diamond from India?" Jillian exclaimed. "You found that, too?"

"Found it, but as of yet, it's unrecovered."

"Who has it?" I asked.

"It's being stored at Cryptex Solutions, isn't it?" Jillian guessed.

Josh nodded. "Yes. I've been working on angles for how I can get in there and get it out. Or force the thief to bring it to me. I have a couple of ideas, I just haven't implemented them. As for Coronado, you've heard of Tucker's Cross?"

The two of us shook our heads no.

"Tucker's Cross is a 22 karat gold cross studded with emeralds. It is single-handedly the most expensive item ever recovered in a shipwreck."

"Someone stole it," I guessed.

"Someone broke into the museum that had it and replaced it with a replica," Josh corrected. "I'm pretty sure it's at Cryptex, too."

"Why call it Coronado?" I asked.

"You've seen *Indiana Jones and the Last Crusade*?"

"Who hasn't?" I countered. "Oh, wait a minute. At the beginning of the movie, a young Indiana Jones steals a cross from the thief who took it in the first place. But, the authorities force him to return it, isn't that right?"

"Right. Indiana Jones recovers it a second time,

this time as an adult. Anyway, that cross reminded me of Tucker's Cross, so the name stuck."

"Hello there," a cheery voice exclaimed.

Sherlock and Watson, who had been snoozing at our feet, perked up. Lestrade reached down and gave each of the dogs a scratch. The three of us rose to our feet.

"Hello, you two," Lestrade continued. "If you weren't famous before, you certainly will be now. Mr. Anderson, Ms. Cooper, good day to you. Lieutenant Cooper, I'm damn glad to see you're doing better."

"Sergeant Major," Josh responded. He waited for Lestrade to nod before taking his seat.

"Wait just a minute," Jillian exclaimed. She looked at Lestrade. "You said you're a detective sergeant."

"I said I was undercover," Lestrade argued, grinning. "At ease, Lieutenant."

"Thank you, sir."

I stared at our British friend as I replayed that scene in my head.

"Lestrade? Are you Josh's boss?"

"Let's just say that I'm responsible for him while he's working for the Crown," Lestrade said, nodding.

"Why do they keep calling you Lestrade, sir?" Josh asked.

Jillian and I rounded on Lestrade.

"Excuse me? Your name isn't Lestrade?"

"It went with Sherlock and Watson. What can I

say? It was the Queen's idea."

"What's your name?" Jillian asked. "Your real name."

"Sergeant Major Davis Forrester, at your service."

"Davis Forrester?" I repeated, frowning. "That's either one mother of a coincidence, or …"

"Don't believe everything you read," Lestrade told us, or should I say, Davis told us. "The Davis Forrester you are familiar with did, in fact, have those two cannons in his possession. However, since the Crown is actively investigating Cryptex Solutions, it was decided to change the name of the perpetrator."

"To your name?" I asked, confused.

Davis shrugged. "I lost a bet. What of it?"

"He has the world's worst luck," Josh laughed.

Davis checked his watch and sighed. "They're late. Very uncharacteristic, if you ask me."

"Who is late?" I wanted to know.

Josh checked his phone. "Not only late, but late by nearly twenty minutes. Then again, they had a lot to set up."

"*Who* had *what* to set up?" I asked, growing irritated.

Right on cue, a sleek dark red limousine pulled into the hotel's main entrance. The driver's door opened and out jumped Mr. Tibbet, the same driver as before. He spotted our group sitting close by and bowed once before extending an arm in invitation.

"What's going on?" Jillian asked. "We're not

supposed to go back to the palace, are we?"

Josh pushed away from the table and rose to his feet. "Nope. I do believe that car is for us. Come on, Jillian."

"Tell me what's going on first," Jillian insisted.

"Trust me, Jay-Jay," Josh said, using a new nickname I had never heard before.

Jillian was hesitant for a few moments before finally following her brother off the patio and toward the car. Mr. Tibbet gave us a broad smile and opened the passenger door as we approached. Jillian entered first, followed immediately by Josh. However, much to my surprise, Mr. Tibbet closed the door before the dogs or I could step inside.

"What's going on?" I asked, confused.

The passenger window rolled down and Josh stuck his head out.

"Don't worry, bro. You're in the next one. Mr. Tibbet? I do believe we're late. You know where to go?"

"I do, sir. And ... we're off."

The maroon Bentley pulled smoothly away from the curb. Turning to Lestrade, er, Davis, I gave him a questioning look.

"Do you know what's going on?"

"Well, maybe."

"Will you tell me what's going on?"

A perfect replica of the first Bentley pulled up to the hotel. I actually leaned down to look through the windows, expecting to see Jillian and Josh, but no. The car was empty. An unfamiliar driver hastily exited and approached. This driver was female, had her brown hair pulled up, into a tight bun, and was wearing the same uniform as Mr. Tibbet. She pulled out a slip of paper and read it aloud.

"One American, holding the leashes to two corgis. Plus, Sergeant Major Forrester will be in attendance. Gentlemen, I have your car. If you will kindly step inside, I'll take you to where you need to be."

"And where do I need to be?" I asked, as I lifted the corgis into the back of the car and took the seat next to Davis. "I don't even know what's going on."

"Think of it as a present from Her Majesty the Queen," Davis offered.

"Look, dude, just tell me what's going on."

"Zachary, haven't you figured it out? You're about to get married."

"I'm about to … excuse me?"

"Oh, don't fret. We've taken care of everything."

"You've taken care of … listen, there's a whole lot of planning that goes into holding a wedding. You might not have realized this, but no one is here but us. We can't get married without our parents here. It'd break their hearts. Thank the Queen for me, but I think I'm going to need to … wait. The Queen brought them all over, didn't she?"

"They're waiting for us at the Abbey."

"Abbey? What Abbey? We aren't supposed to get married in an Abbey. We decided against holding it anywhere with a religious background."

"How's Westminster sound?" Davis asked, giving me a huge grin.

"Westminster? We're getting married in Westminster Abbey? Isn't that where …?"

"Prince William and Catherine Middleton were married, yes."

"What the …? Are you sure that's even allowed?"

"Express permission given by Her Majesty the Queen," Davis confirmed.

"And does Jillian know this?"

"I'm sure she does by now. Come on. You can't show up at Westminster Abbey looking like that."

"Where are we going?"

"We're going to make you presentable."

"I don't care how good your people are. There's no way you're going to be able to find a tuxedo that fits me in such a short amount of time."

"I think you underestimate who you're talking to," Davis said, in mock-seriousness. "Leave that to us. Look, we're here. Give me the leashes. I'll show you where they're all waiting for you."

The next hour disappeared in the blink of an eye. When Davis had said *they*, he hadn't been messing around. I felt like one of those race cars, and I had just walked into a highly-trained pit crew. A hair stylist actually trimmed my hair and a guy with a razor gave me my first ever shave performed by someone other than myself. And as long as we were talking about firsts, a team of two women, one on either hand, gave me my first ever manicure.

"Seriously? Is all of this really necessary?"

"You only get married once," one of the women told me, with a smile. "You will want to look your best, love."

"This would be my second, actually," I admitted.

The woman working on my left hand gave me a sheepish grin. "Second time's the charm, is it?"

I could really make her feel bad and tell her I was widowed, but the bizarreness of the situation was making me smile. Here I was, getting measured and fitted for a tuxedo that was literally being assembled before my very eyes. I was told the entire process would typically take at least three hours of solid work, by some of the most gifted tailors London had at its disposal. In my case, it took a team of four about forty-five minutes, but with everything that was happening, it was over in no time flat. All I could think about was that I was going to be able to marry Jillian, and yes, the circumstances may have been extraordinary, but the only thing I could think about was finally tying the knot with the woman who had stolen my heart.

"Can't wait to see her, huh?" Davis teased, giving me a friendly pat on the back. "I'm told they pulled out all the stops in getting her ready."

"I'd just like to know how she took the news about all of this," I said, with a nervous chuckle.

"Probably the same as you," Davis said, grinning.

"Face this way, please," one of the tailors requested.

"Where are the dogs?" I asked.

"Being fitted, same as you."

"Wh-what? You're kidding!"

"Not at all. Her Majesty assumed you'd like to include Sherlock and Watson, so they're getting properly fitted, too."

"Umm, you don't understand. The dogs absolutely *hate* wearing outfits. Learned that the hard way one Halloween a while back."

"Really? I thought they looked rather regal in their attire, as though this isn't the first time they've been dressed up."

"What? No way."

"See for yourself."

"Where are they?"

"Over there, near the window."

Turning, I saw a sight which made me laugh out loud. There were the dogs, wearing doggie jackets which, amazingly enough, matched the one I was now wearing. The soft black cotton stretched the full length of their backs and made them both look quite dashing. The reason I laughed, though, is that each of the dogs was also getting a manicure, so to speak. Their nails were trimmed, a stylist was running brushes through the parts of their coats not covered by their tuxedo-jackets, and if I didn't know any better, then I'd say both corgis were having the time of their lives. Little snots. Not only do they both hate bath day, Sherlock and Watson liken the act of nail trimming to taking their medicines. Thankfully, trying to sneak a pill into a dog didn't happen very often.

With the three of us looking the best we ever have, we were bundled back into our limousine and rushed to Westminster Abbey. As you probably know, this particular abbey has seen its fair share of royal weddings. Prince Albert and Lady Elizabeth Bowes-Lyon, in 1923; Princess Elizabeth (the future Queen) and Lieutenant Philip Mountbatten, in 1947; and Prince William and Catherine Middleton, in 2011, to name a few. And coronations! Westminster Abbey has been the site of all royal coronations since the 11th century! This was where Her Majesty the Queen was coronated, in 1953. Now, it was going to be where Jillian and I were married! Let's see if anyone we know will be able to top *this* particular story!

The last wedding ceremony I mentioned was enough to have my mind spinning, especially as we pulled up to the abbey. While I don't really follow the lives of the British royal family, I knew Jillian did, so she must be beyond excited. I just didn't know what we were going to tell all our friends back home. You know, the ones who had been planning on being able to attend? I didn't want them to think that we were trying to blow them off.

"We should have a ... yes, there they are," Davis observed, as the limousine stopped beside a group of five people.

"Right this way, sir," I was told, as the car doors were held open. "Such adorable dogs."

Davis suddenly snapped his fingers. "That's right. Sherlock and Watson have their places to be, too. So, hand me their leashes. Good. Now, I'll see you shortly. You're going that way, and the dogs and I are going *this* way."

I turned to watch the dogs, but they had their backs to me and were walking alongside Davis. Neither dog, I'd like to point out, bothered to look back at me. Man's best friend, huh?

"Zack!" I heard a familiar voice exclaim. "Bro! Look out, people, Best Man is coming through."

A smile split my face as I saw Harrison Watt, PV veterinarian and my best friend, pushing his way through the crowd of people milling about. Harry had also been my best friend in high school, and somehow, the planets aligned for the two of us to end up in the same small Oregon town. I should have known the Queen had all the bases covered.

"Pretty swank, pal," another voice said. There, behind Harry, was my good friend Vance Samuelson, police detective extraordinaire from Pomme Valley. "Heard you've been having all kinds of fun here without us. What's that all about?"

"Well, it …" I began.

"I'm just messing with you. Wow. You sure know how to make friends, don't you?"

"Can't help notice that you two are both dressed for the occasion," I observed, giving both of my friends a smile.

"You, too, pal," Vance returned. "It's not often a strange English dude shows up at your door and hands you tickets to fly across the Atlantic."

"Older guy?" I asked. "Accent, drives a big Bentley? Yeah, we had the same guy."

"Who, that old geezer who sounded like a butler?" Harry asked, overhearing.

I sighed. "Yep, that's the one. Glad you made it, guys."

"You don't say no to the Queen, bro," Harry said, waggling a finger at me.

"Where's Tori?" I wanted to know. "And Julie? What about the kids?"

"They're all here, bro," Harry assured me. "Tori and Julie are bridesmaids, and the kids are all sitting together."

We caught sight of someone in a uniform waving at us. Curious, we headed over.

"They're ready to begin, sir. If you and your groomsmen would kindly step through there?"

I don't know if you were lucky enough to see the streamed coverage of Prince William's and Catherine Middleton's wedding, but as I mentioned before, it was also held here, at Westminster Abbey. Seriously, this one place has so much history attached to it that it literally boggles the mind. At least, it did for me.

Following my two friends into the Abbey, I was surprised to learn this church could easily seat two thousand people. Granted, there weren't that many people in attendance today, but still, I'd have to say that at least a third of the pews were occupied, only I didn't recognize anyone. Other than Harry and Vance, of course. But, that changed once I walked past the front rows. My parents were there with my siblings' children, waving enthusiastically at me as I passed.

Clara Cooper, Jillian's mother, was seated a little further to the right, with an empty space next to her, of course. There, in his full dress blues, complete with white canvas belt and ceremonial sword, was First Sergeant Joshua Cooper, looking remarkably refreshed since I saw him last, which was ... oh, less than an hour ago.

A round of laughter and applause erupted as the ring bearer and flower girl arrived. I'm pretty sure both Sherlock and Watson strutted their way down the aisle, stopping to look up and sniff each row they passed. Pictures were taken and the dogs received more than their fair share of pats on the head. It was at this time when I noticed who was sitting between my parents and Jillian's: Her Majesty the Queen. The Queen of England was actually attending our wedding!

Sherlock and Watson stopped at the front row to look at the Queen. The moment they did, practically everyone present snapped a few pictures. The applause coming from the attendees was loud enough to shake the rafters. Giving the Queen's outstretched hand a gentle lick, Sherlock and Watson then proceeded to join me at the altar. After a few moments, they settled down to watch the proceedings.

I have to tell you my mind was pretty much blown by this point. There were way, way too many things to process. However, if I thought I was lacking on the little gray cells, as a famous Belgian detective was fond of saying, it paled in comparison to what happened once Jillian and her bridesmaids made their appearance. Her closest friends from PV slowly made their way down the aisle: Tori, Julie, Hannah, and Taylor. Then, much to my surprise, I saw my own sister, Kira, beaming a smile at me as she took her place in Jillian's entourage. Then, the entire church fell silent as the Bridal Chorus began to play. And that was also about the time I noticed that the music wasn't being piped in anywhere, but was coming from an actual live orchestra, stationed off to the left.

"Like the dress?" Harry asked, as he leaned conspiratorially at me. "Jules said that it's one of the most sought-after styles out there, and it was custom-fitted to her by the actual designer of the dress."

I know Harry was talking, but quite literally, I lost the ability to form coherent thoughts the moments my fiancée had appeared.

"They say it's worth nearly two hundred thousand pounds," Harry continued. "See the sweetheart neckline? And all those sparkles? They're Swarovski crystals, man. And check out the train! It's gotta be, what, over ten feet long? Jillian must be having the time of her life!"

He was right, though. Jillian was all smiles as she slowly walked down the aisle. Her dress, Jillian later confirmed, was from a top designer. The mermaid style gown had a natural waistline, an off the shoulder sweetheart neckline, and a cathedral train. The fabric, which looked airy and light, was something called misty tulle. And wow, those Swarovski crystals, which sparkled across the bodice of the dress, were stunning.

After Harry successfully pointed out several of these observations, I finally turned to my friend. "How the blazes do you know so much about wedding dresses?"

"You can thank Tori for that. Turns out they've been working on that dress, non-stop, for several days straight."

That caught my attention.

"Wait, that means they knew we were going to be married here? Looks like the two of us were the last to know. Hey, how long have you been here?"

"We took a red-eye," Harry said. "We left on Saturday, and arrived on Sunday. What a trip, bro."

I held out a hand. "Glad you're here, pal."

Harry pumped my hand. "Anytime, bro. Anytime."

I looked down the line at my groomsmen. Harry, Vance, my brother, Barry, and seeing how I was a couple of groomsmen short, my father and my new friend, Lestrade. Er, make that Davis Forrester.

They say Catholic wedding ceremonies are way too long, but I wouldn't know. I barely remember any of the ceremony itself, seeing how I had been rendered mute the moment Jillian and her father walked down the aisle. Wyatt Cooper reached the altar, gently pulled Jillian's veil back, and gave his daughter a kiss on the cheek. He shook my hand and then took his place next to his wife, which was also, coincidentally enough, next to the Queen. I found out later that Westminster Abbey is an Anglican church, and the only people who could get married there were members of the Royal Family, a member of the Order of Bath, or anyone who lives within the Abbey's precincts. The simple fact that we, two Americans, were allowed to tie the knot here was a testament to how much power and sway the Queen held.

With Jillian's arm hooked through mine, I started to turn around, so I could face the priest, when I caught sight of something that made my heart swell even further. The Queen had thought of everything. A huge flat-panel television was on the far wall, and it was showing me a live-action stream of ... you guessed it, Pomme Valley. I was looking inside the high school auditorium, and I should mention that, once I made eye contact with the screen and raised a hand in greeting, the entire gathering of people, which had filled that auditorium, by the way, jumped to their feet and began cheering.

With our vows exchanged, the priest announced to everyone present—and those back home in Oregon—we were now Mr. and Mrs. Zachary Anderson. Smiling and holding up our clasped hands, which showed off the rings we picked out for each other, the two of us smiled and waved at our friends before turning to Her Majesty. I gave her a slight neck bow, while Jillian executed a perfect curtsy. Then, holding the hand of my beautiful wife, we walked down the aisle, amidst the cheering of strangers, family, friends, and what had to be the entire town of Pomme Valley. Fortune was smiling on me a second time, and I wasn't about to waste it.

Life is good.

AUTHOR'S NOTE

There are varying reports of what size the Cullinan diamond happens to be. I've seen 530.2 and 530.4 carats. Well, I went with the first number I found, which had the point two at the end. You'd also think that creating a math equation isn't that difficult, but I can attest it's a bigger pain than you might think. So, if the Cullinan happens to be the 530.4, well, I humbly apologize, but I am *not* coming up with a different equation. The first will do.

If you have never been to England, and experienced London for yourself, I wholeheartedly recommend it. My wife and I celebrated our 20th anniversary with a cruise around the British Isles. It was the first time for either of us in Europe, and we made the best of it. England, Scotland, Ireland, Wales, Northern Ireland, and France. We loved it.

All right, what's next? Well, for the Corgi Case Files, we're returning to PV for *Case of the Stuttering Parrot*. Little Ruby has suddenly started spouting some gibberish, only … is it? I'm also starting *Strike the Spark* (DoA2), which is the second book in my new fantasy series. With the world already created, and the characters having back stories, this should go a whole lot smoother than last time.

If you enjoyed the book, please consider leaving a review wherever you purchased it. Reviews are worth their weight in gold for us authors. Never miss another new release! Sign up for my newsletter, which can be found on my website: www.AuthorJMPoole.com.

Be safe out there! Happy reading!

J.

Zack and the dogs will return, in
Case of the Stuttering Parrot
(Corgi Case Files #15), Early 2022

* * *

Meanwhile, catch up on the entire
Corgi Case Files Series

Available in e-book and paperback
Case of the One-Eyed Tiger
Case of the Fleet-Footed Mummy
Case of the Holiday Hijinks
Case of the Pilfered Pooches
Case of the Muffin Murders
Case of the Chatty Roadrunner
Case of the Highland House Haunting
Case of the Ostentatious Otters
Case of the Dysfunctional Daredevils
Case of the Abandoned Bones
Case of the Great Cranberry Caper
Case of the Shady Shamrock
Case of the Ragin' Cajun
Case of the Missing Marine
*Case of the Stuttering Parrot – coming
in early 2022*

If you enjoy Epic Fantasy, check out Jeff's other series:
Pirates of Perz
Tales of Lentari
Bakkian Chronicles

Made in the USA
Middletown, DE
31 January 2022